Playing Without the Ball

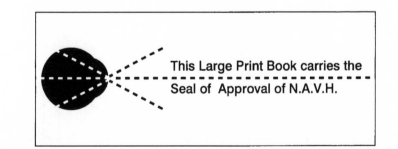

This Large Print Book carries the
Seal of Approval of N.A.V.H.

Playing Without the Ball

A Novel in Four Quarters

Rich Wallace

Thorndike Press • Waterville, Maine

Published in 2001 by arrangement with Random House Children's Books, a division of Random House, Inc.

Thorndike Press Large Print Young Adult Series.

The tree indicium is a trademark of Thorndike Press.

The text of this Large Print edition is unabridged.
Other aspects of the book may vary from the original edition.

Set in 16 pt. Plantin.

Printed in the United States on permanent paper.

Library of Congress Control Number: 2001 131984
ISBN 0-7862-3522-5 (lg. print : hc : alk. paper)

I could make a long list of women who have nurtured and supported me, but I'll dedicate this book to these: my mother and her mother; my sisters, Carol and Lynda.

Singing, each to each.

Thank you, Sandra Neil. I'll love you forever.

And to Tracy Gates, my editor at Knopf. I don't know how to begin to thank you. Maybe by writing more books.

Thank you, Tracy.

If you chase two rabbits, both will escape.

Asian proverb

Contents

ONE

Against the Sky

The wind catches you by surprise when you turn the corner onto Main Street in Sturbridge, Pennsylvania. It's brisker than you expect, and in your face if you turn off a half-deserted side street and head up toward the post office or Rite-Aid or the Turkey Hill convenience store. Especially in late autumn.

It's the week before Halloween, getting dark in a hurry, so Rite-Aid is busy with people picking up giant bags of miniature candy bars and little kids scoping out masks and plastic jack-o'-lanterns. The rest of the stores are mostly closed for the night, but the pizza place is busy and the music store is hanging on for another hour or so. Nobody's in there except the clerk guy with long stringy hair, reading a magazine behind the counter. You can get used CDs for five bucks.

The diner's open across the street, but on this side the gun shop is closed, and Sid's clothing store just shut its lights a couple of seconds ago.

I turn into the alley between Shorty's Bar and Foley's Pizza. The alley is just barely wide enough for Shorty's twenty-year-old blue pickup, but you can squeeze past it if you have reason to take a short-cut over to Church Street. You go around back to reach the steps up to the apartments.

There are four doors up here. The one marked number 3 is mine, just a room with bare walls and a scuffed hardwood floor. The bathroom is painted mint green and has a stand-up shower stall and an oval mirror above the sink.

I sleep on a mattress in the corner; I can't afford a bed yet. I've got a closet, but I also hang clothes on my chair, especially wet stuff like my basketball shorts.

I get free rent. Not exactly free — I work it off in Shorty's kitchen three or four nights a week. The deal includes meals during work hours and five dollars an hour off the books.

When I moved into this place in September, I was seventeen. I'd never had sex, never used drugs, never forgiven my mother, never been to church, and never been a basketball star.

I guess that's all still true.

I played like hell last night — telegraphing my passes, missing layups. That's the sort of thing that eats at me until I get a chance to redeem myself. I heard there's a 6 A.M. game on Tuesdays at the Y, so I set my alarm for 5:30 and stumbled out the door.

Six older guys and a girl about my age — I don't know her; she's new in town — are shooting around when I get there.

"You in?" a tall, bald, old-as-my-father guy asks me.

"Sure."

"You, me, and these two," he says, pointing to my teammates. "Cover my daughter."

I smile a little. She's dribbling the ball at the top of the key. I've seen her around school. Cute. An inch or so taller than me, short blond hair. "Hi," she says.

"Hey."

"I'm Dana."

"Jay."

She passes the ball in and I turn to double up on the pivot guy. Dana cuts to the hoop on a give-and-go, takes a little flip pass, and lays it off the backboard and in.

I play back this time, guarding against

the inside pass. She dribbles once, sets up from fifteen feet and shoots, hitting nothing but net.

I blush a little. "I ain't awake yet," I say.

"Right," she answers, looking me straight in the eyes.

I guard her tighter now, trying not to hack her. She's very quick. Very agile and sleek.

She drifts into the key, thinking she can post up on me, but one of her teammates has dribbled into the corner. He's trapped — double-teamed — with his back to the basket, but he's still trying to dribble his way out.

"Oh, dear," she mutters, close enough to my face that I smell peppermint. She gives me a kind of smirk, a half-look that elevates me. "Dribbling is bad," she says.

"Tell me about it."

The ball goes out of bounds. It's ours.

I stay inside. The ball comes to me. I try to back her toward the basket. She plays me tight; front of her thighs against the back of mine. I give a head fake and drive. She gets a hand on the ball, affecting my dribble, but I recover, spin, and lay it over her outstretched hand. It scores.

Listen to this dream I was having when

my alarm went off this morning.

I'm at the diner and I'm finishing my third consecutive meal. All of them were chicken dishes; the first two were the same, the third somewhat different. I can't recall the exact meals, but the chicken seemed to be fried and had thick gravy on it. I kept ordering dinners because I was hoping the waitress I had would go on a break and the more enticing new one would take over. But that didn't happen. Plus, I was very hungry.

Eventually I got up to pay, timing it so the preferred waitress would be at the register. I remember saying to her that I'd made a pig of myself.

I paid with a twenty, and I needed two more dollars. I started digging in my wallet but I couldn't find any singles, even though I knew they were in there. There was an elderly guy on line behind me, and he said he'd give me the money. I said no, I have it, but thanks anyway. Then I managed to spill everything in my wallet (in fact, far more stuff than I possibly could have carried in my wallet — my report card, a couple of golf balls, the lyric sheet from an Allman Brothers CD, a naked G.I. Joe doll, and a thousand pennies) all over the counter and the floor. As I was picking it up, the waitress who had served me came over and punched me on the shoulder and said, "Nice going, Jay, that guy behind you just died." I stood up, kind of stunned, and she looked at me in disbelief and said, "*Help* him!"

Well, the guy hadn't died, but he was shriveled up and could barely talk, and he said he'd had a heart attack. The nicer waitress was propping him up. I said, "I'll get some ice." [Note: This would have been a useless gesture.]

So I ran into the kitchen, gathered up a huge batch of ice, and then (holding the armload of ice) started trying to open cabinets and drawers to find a plastic bag to put it in.

That's when my alarm went off.

Game point, 6–6. She sets a screen at the foul line, and I'm not sure of the protocol for fighting through an opposite-gender pick.

"Come on," she says softly, "use it." But the guy dribbles toward the corner again. Same guy, same corner. This time he's open.

"That's you," she says, still whispering, like she's announcing the game to herself. "Oh, dear," she says as he halts his dribble and starts looking around. "Gotta shoot that."

Instead the guy tries to force a pass back to her, but it's way too high. She gets a hand on it, but no way she can recover. I grab the ball, step behind the arc, and shoot.

"Shit," I hear her say as it goes in.

About time.

Basketball Reality

Big crowd on Saturday night. On week-nights Shorty's gets middle-aged regulars, guys who come in to shoot pool after work at Sturbridge Building Products and drink pints of Yeungling or Coors. Those nights I'm mostly frying hamburgers. But the group shifts way younger on Fridays and Saturdays if Shorty brings in a band. Then I'm cooking a lot of wings.

Spit's band is on tonight, so the fat guys in cowboy hats get to stare at skinny, barely legal women with breast tattoos. The noise level is high, and every five minutes or so somebody stumbles into the kitchen by mistake, expecting it to be a bathroom.

It's about 10 when Shorty hollers for me to bring up a case of Molson.

"Extradite it," he says.

"Extra what?"

"Extradite. Quickly. Chop chop."

So I pass through the bar room, checking out the clientele. I stay in back as much as possible because Shorty could get screwed for letting me handle alcohol. But I have to leave the kitchen to get to the cellar, so I squeeze through the crowd and cut behind the bar.

You have to watch your head as you walk up the creaky wooden steps with the beer. Bobbi spots me and smiles. "They cold?" she asks.

"Yeah."

Bobbi is about twenty-five and built, and she tends bar with Shorty on weekends. She takes one of the Molsons from the case and sets it on the bar in front of a landscaper named Chris, a beefy guy with curly blond hair in a Lynyrd Skynyrd T-shirt. He's married, but spends most of his nights on this bar stool. Bobbi smiles and sticks her tongue between her teeth as she opens the bottle.

"Dee-licious," Chris says as Bobbi pours it into a glass.

"You haven't tasted it yet," she says.

"I don't mean the beer," he says, winking at her.

Bobbi is every guy's fantasy in here and she knows how to flirt just enough to keep them interested. I watch her for a few minutes, drawing beers, smiling when they make their lame jokes about taking her home. You have to just about shout to be heard above the band, and above everybody else who's shouting, too.

Shorty catches my eye and motions with his head for me to get out of sight. I nod. I go.

The first time I entered Shorty's Bar was Labor Day weekend, almost two months ago. Me and my dad had reached a stalemate — I wasn't going to California and my father definitely was.

We'd been through this every night for about two months. My father had a "job offer" out in Los Angeles that he couldn't pass up. The job was managing the breakfast shift at a Denny's — with a promotion soon if it works out. Mostly he just needed to get away from here.

I'll get into that later. The abbreviated version is that, realistically, I have one season of basketball left and this is the only town I can use it in. No way I walk into a school in L.A. as a scrawny white senior and make the team. So we compromised. I'd rent this room from Shorty DiGiorgio — the only guy around with any use for my father — and Shorty would watch out for me like a hired uncle or something. Then in June I'd pack up and join my dad out west.

Shorty stuck to the watch-out-for-Jay deal for about two days. Since then, I'm pretty much doing whatever I want to.

Shorty is a man who does not give a shit. He rakes in money from this bar and from taking bets on sporting events. He liked my father because he was a major contributor to both sources of income.

Here's the basketball reality. I'm a borderline player, but at least I'm a known entity in this town. The coaches know I've run my ass off ever since the Biddy League back in fourth grade, even if my shooting touch is less than consistent.

I'm about five-foot-eight, with good speed and strong legs. My style on the court can be deceptively smooth — simple but effective passes inside, more rebounds than a guy my size ought to get. But making the varsity is not a lock. If you're not going to be an impact player as a senior, then you just aren't going to stick.

I see it. Why keep a non-contributing senior when you can develop a younger guy instead?

I see it, but it sucks. If I was a coach, I'd never screw a kid who'd worked his butt off for so long. But a senior is far more likely to get the ax than an underclassman.

So I have to be twice as good to stay.

The thing about basketball is that it gets into your head real easy. Sturbridge is not a place where hoops has ever been big; high school wrestling is a town-wide obsession and that team is always among the best in Pennsylvania. But basketball has caught on here lately, more on the recreational level than scholastically. It's fueled by the general desire for fitness, I suppose, but it goes a lot deeper than that. I've played enough with everybody — the doctors and lawyers who play like stegosaurs on Sunday afternoons, the playground boys who'd never go near a real team but can play their asses off anyway, the hard-core guys with beer guts and bad knees who play in the men's league — to figure out the socio-dynamic crap.

The Sturbridge YMCA runs men's basketball leagues most of the year, using outdoor courts through the summer, but moving to late-evening hours inside the Y's narrow, rickety gym from October through April. The men's league has teams sponsored by bars and insurance agencies and pizzerias, and the rare opening on a roster is quickly filled with somebody's buddy or a recent high school player who's kept himself in shape.

There's also the forty-and-older league, which has a slower pace but only a few less fights and hard fouls. And there are pickup games going on whenever there's open gym time at the Y. I've been spending as many hours there as I can, mixing in with whoever's on the court. You learn the pecking order pretty quickly, moving up over time if you're into it.

The high school program is proud but undistinguished, run by Ralph "Buddy" Johnson, a gym teacher in his forties who played forward here a long time ago and is dead serious about the game. But he's been coaching for twenty years and has only had four winning seasons. One league championship sixteen years ago — the banner is hanging from the ceiling above midcourt.

"We play clean, unselfish basketball here," Johnson tells us every year at the tryouts. "None of that Harlem playground shit in my gym."

Last year the varsity won just seven games, mostly on the shoulders of all-conference point guard Brian Kaipo. Some say the game has passed Johnson by. Others say it had a mighty big head start.

I'm scraping burnt grease off the grill when the sound of Spit's voice stops me cold. She's singing an autobiographical tune about being alone and bewildered, something I don't think she's over yet. I set down the spatula, wipe my hands on my white cook's shirt, and lean against the doorway to watch the band for a few minutes.

All potential goes to nothing
Anoint or you'll annoy

If you concentrate, you can hear a trace of the Mediterranean in her voice, beneath the Newark and the punk and the confusion. There's an athleticism in her wired frenzy, her ropy black hair swinging against her shoulders, and her pale stomach showing when her shirt whips about on the stage.

Feed your ego, feed your soul
Create or you'll destroy

Something, the knotty strength in her legs maybe, makes you believe that she really could have been a gymnast, back before her growth and her addictions and her anger.

Spit. For Sarita. The most unlikely

friend I've ever had.

She's almost twenty, spent a year at Tyler School of Art, lived with one of her instructors in Philadelphia since the middle of the first semester — some guy named James. He broke her heart last spring so she came to Sturbridge where her mother had landed after finally going through with the divorce.

Spit's working as a legal assistant. "It sucks," she says, "but it supports my excesses."

Her excesses, the obvious ones, are energy, hair color (streaks of orange in the natural black), emotion (approaching both extremes), and intelligence. She's the lead singer, songwriter, and apparent brains of the rock group Elyit, which formed within a week of her arrival in town. They play at Shorty's about three times a month, but so far have not landed any other "gigs."

Bobbi brings in the predictable run of orders around 11:30 when guys who've been drinking for three hours get the munchies. Four cheese steaks, three orders of fries, and a hamburger.

"And somebody broke a bottle over by the jukebox, when you get a chance," she says.

I clean up the bottle before starting on the orders, brushing the bits of glass into a dustpan. The bar room is long and tight, and a guy backs into my head when I'm bent over. About eight people are dancing on the tiny dance floor, but most of the customers are standing around, packed in close, looking for somebody to go home with. I know how they feel.

The band is taking a break; the dancers are blundering to "Satisfaction," which is playing in my ear from the jukebox as I wipe the gritty floor with a towel.

The place closes at 2. Shorty limps into the kitchen about 2:15. (Shorty has told people the injury is from Vietnam; at other times he's said it happened playing football. People who know him best say he was just born with a left leg that's two inches shorter than his right.)

"I'm out of here," he says. "Don't forget the bathroom floors."

"I won't," I say. I know how much urine a weekend crowd can spill. "Have a good night?"

"Great night," Shorty says. "They ain't bad." Spit's group he means. "They bring people in."

There aren't many local options if you

want live entertainment. Shorty's can accommodate fifty customers without too much squeezing, but there were at least seventy packed in here tonight.

"Anyway," Shorty says. "See you tomorrow."

I wipe down the stovetop and pour some ammonia in a bucket. I'll mop the bathrooms real quick. I'll mop the toilets, too. No way I'm getting any closer than that.

I push the ladies' room door open with my foot and take a step back in surprise.

"Spit," I say. She's sitting on the back of the toilet, up on the tank.

"I'm spaced," she says.

"Oh."

She stands up and wobbles.

"You all right?" I ask.

"Yeah. A guy gave me some acid. I haven't done acid in ages."

Great. I'm alone in the bar with a hallucinating woman.

"Shocking, huh?" she says, noting my expression. "It's no big deal, bud. Come on, let's go for a walk."

I figure I can mop up tomorrow — Shorty doesn't open until 3 on Sundays.

"Just till I come down," she says.

"Okay."

We step out the back door. The air is

cold and still. Nothing is open; no one is out.

"Oooh," she says. "I can breathe again."

I take a deep inhale, kind of in agreement. We walk through the car dealership lot on Church Street and head for the park.

"You don't seem too high," I say.

"I'm not. It's like an intense focus right about here," she says, putting her palms up to her forehead. "Everything else is just sort of fuzzy."

I nod, as if I can relate.

"I've still got a hit if you want it," she says.

I shake my head. No way.

The park covers one large block in front of the courthouse. There's a fountain in the middle and diagonal sidewalk paths going from corner to corner. There are a few benches, a few trees, and a couple of pieces of playground equipment. We sit on a bench halfway between the fountain and the street.

"You sang good tonight," I say.

She raises her eyebrows. "I guess," she says. "For a few minutes there I felt like we were clicking." She stretches both arms out and yawns. "This town isn't exactly hip."

She's got her feet tucked up on the

bench and is hugging her knees. Both legs of her jeans are ripped at the knees.

"My moments of clarity come by once a week if I'm lucky," she says. "When I get my mind off James. See, I'm usually terrified, like I'll just fade away, like I'm losing my grip, and I'll get farther and farther from that inner voice and never get it back."

I'm trying to keep up with her. My primary concerns are basketball and getting enough to eat, so I'm listening to her and comparing it to my own life, and she's just rambling like it doesn't even matter if I'm sitting there.

She's picking at the threads by her knee. "I get down," she says. "I worry. And then this goofy optimism kicks in and makes me search for that next rush in spite of myself." She draws a counterclockwise circle in the air.

I'm freezing my ass off. "You coming down?" I ask.

"Maybe some," she says. "We can go."

She sings softly as we walk back, some Portuguese folk song she learned from her mom. A police car goes by and slows a little, then moves along.

We reach the back steps and she puts a hand on my shoulder. "Can I crash here?" she says.

I think about it for a second. I've got a sleeping bag in the closet. "There's not much room," I say.

"I don't need much."

When I come out of the bathroom, Spit is passed out on the mattress. I open the closet door to get the sleeping bag, but she wakes up and says, "Just get in."

I shrug and get under the blanket. She rolls onto her side and says good night.

I hunch up on the side of the bed. I prefer to sleep facedown, with all four limbs spread, but I'm so tired I don't give a shit. Spit's asleep again already. I can smell her dried sweat; her breath is raspy and sour.

This is the first woman I've ever slept with, literally or figuratively. But it's hardly a moment to treasure.

WHAT'S MISSING

Ethnicity? I suppose we had some, three or four generations back, but it's been bleached out of us pretty good. We're as white as Twinkies and fish sticks.

It's a neutral, Wonder Bread sort of whiteness, a bland-talking, straight-thinking, virginal whiteness. Like Cheerios.

When I was little, before my mother took off, she'd buy those cartons of vanilla, chocolate, and strawberry ice cream. She'd dish it up and I'd let it get soft, and I'd experiment with mixtures, stirring different combinations together. And it struck me that if you added just a drop of melted chocolate to a dish full of vanilla, the mix would take on an undebatable tone of brown. But stir a drop of vanilla into a spoonful of chocolate and you'd never even know it was there.

I play basketball. Every day. At school, at the Y, in people's driveways. My game is sound, but it's quiet and unremarkable. That's attitude. Or the absence of it. I've got a white man's game in a black man's sport.

I bet my great-great-grandfather kicked some ass on the boat over here from Glasgow. But the McLeods have gone downhill from there.

I need to find myself some attitude.

Sunday morning I sleep too late, waking with a start. Spit opens her eyes, wipes her nose with her fist, and burrows back under the blanket. I bolt some orange juice and a package of Yodels, brush my teeth, and jog over to the Y.

I can hear the springy thud of a basketball as I rush up the steps, a sign that the games are under way.

A guy named Eddie is sitting on the bottom row of the bleachers. "Jay," he says, nodding to me. "They need one down that end." I hustle to the other side of the gym.

The first twenty-four guys to show up are in. Anybody who gets here after that has to wait for an opening. Today I'm the twenty-fourth to arrive.

You put three teams of four players at both baskets and they play a continual round-robin format. Play two games, sit one. Winners out: you score, you keep the ball.

The gym is small and cramped and it's all old wood — wooden backboards, wooden bleachers. You go three feet out of bounds on any side of the court and you collide with a wall or the seats. It's usually too hot in here, but on cold winter days you get a wicked breeze sneaking through.

"Guess you're with us," says an older guy with wraps on both knees. The other two players waiting are on the small side, too: Mr. Mendoza, who gave me a C-minus in algebra my freshman year, and a thin, brush-cut sophomore named Jerry.

"Looks like we got four guards," I say.

"We'll run on 'em," says the guy with the knees. "I'm Mike." He sticks out his hand.

"Jay."

There's a lot of beef out there, and the half-court game pretty much negates any speed advantage we might have. But what the hell. I cover a six-foot-four guy about thirty in the first game and I can't stop him for shit. I don't care. You get your ass kicked in a game like this, but you can't help picking up a thing or two that will help sometime. Whatever level you get to, there's always going to be someone better.

We lose 7–2, but I'm warm now, ready to play.

The other team comes on and we match

up better heightwise. I cover Dr. DiPisa, a urologist who's about my size except for his gut. He pushes and grabs a lot, sets moving picks. But he's easy to frustrate. I make some sharp cuts, get a few backdoor layups. Mike starts hitting from outside and we win 7–5.

It's our turn to sit.

"Lenny's playing his usual clean game, I see," says Mike.

"Who?"

"DiPisa. The guy thinks it's a wrestling match."

"No big deal," I say. "I'm a lot quicker than him."

Mr. Mendoza takes a towel out of his gym bag and wipes his face. "He does that shit to everybody," he says. "He's a wimp. We'll just nail him with a couple of picks."

I suddenly remember that Mendoza ran against DiPisa for council last year and lost. Democrats never win in this town.

We go to a zone next game in an effort to clog the lane and slow down the big guy. It works some, but we foul a lot. We manage to tie it at six, and you can feel the intensity pick up another notch.

They bring the ball in and Mendoza and I double-team the big man. Somebody has to be open. A shot goes up from the baseline and grazes off the rim. Mendoza gets a hand on it, but the big guy takes it away and lays it in.

"Son of a bitch," Mendoza says.

The guy raises a fist and they walk off the court. They haven't lost yet.

Dr. DiPisa's team comes back on and immediately goes up 3–0 on us.

"Settle down," Mike says. "Play some D."

DiPisa's trying to drive on me, but I hold my ground. Mendoza doubles up on him and swipes the ball away, runs it down, and makes a nice needle-threading pass to me for a layup. Mike hits a long jumper, then Jerry scores to tie it up.

Mike inbounds the ball to me and I dribble outside with DiPisa guarding me tight. I see Mendoza drifting toward the foul line, so I feint right and drive left. DiPisa runs straight into Mendoza's pick, and Mendoza adds a bit of elbow to his face. I hit the jumper.

DiPisa rubs his jaw and calls Mendoza an asshole. Mendoza just smirks and calls for the ball at the top of the key.

They never get it back. We win 7–3.

"Let me cover DiPisser next game," Mr. Mendoza says to me while we sit. "He'll be so concerned about getting even with me that he'll just drive and take bad shots."

We finally get a win over the big guys, so we're on a roll. DiPisa's team comes back on and has decided to make it physical. They've dropped five straight games and have nothing to lose. DiPisa stays on me even though I cover someone else.

I try to avoid calling fouls, but he hacks me bad on two consecutive drives and I have to say I got it. Mendoza catches my eye and squints sort of hard, and I read that as an indication that he'll take him out this time. Same play as before: a quick fake and a move toward the foul line. Mendoza gives me a screen with something extra for DiPisa. I hear the collision, make the shot. Next thing I know DiPisa's taking a swing and Mendoza is holding his mouth.

Mendoza swings back before they're separated, a couple of guys holding each of them.

It takes a few minutes for things to settle down. Eventually they shake hands and laugh about it.

"Latin blood," says DiPisa. "That's all it is."

"We've been at each other since seventh grade," says Mendoza. "One of these days we'll grow up."

Restless Nights

Sturbridge is in this valley about thirty miles east of Scranton, up in the northeasternmost county in Pennsylvania. There's less than 5,000 people in the actual town, but the school district is huge, so we're pulling in kids from way up by the New York border. Most guys seem to work over at Sturbridge Building Products, which is a big plant that makes things like cinder blocks and concrete septic tanks. My father put in some time there, but he's never held any job for very long.

Sturbridge High School is one of only four in the county, so we travel to compete in the Greater Scranton Scholastic League. We dominate in wrestling and sometimes win it all in football or baseball. Basketball never seems to cut it.

The stores on Main Street sort of struggle by, relying on regulars and tourists. Most people do their bigger shopping out at the Kmart or in the malls over toward Scranton.

There are five taverns on the six-block stretch of downtown Main Street, with Shorty's smack in the middle.

It's early evening. Spit is sitting on a stool in the kitchen smoking a cigarette, while I put together a Reuben sandwich. Her band practices here from 5 to 7 on Mondays, when the place is empty. Then she'll hang around the kitchen until she gets bored.

"Thought you quit," I say.

"I did. Cigarettes suck."

She rolls up a leg of her pants and starts rubbing her shin.

"What'd you do?" I ask.

"It just aches sometimes after a gig or a practice," she says. "I won a gymnastics tournament when I was eleven, and the girl who came in second kicked me in the locker room. Cracked it. Some bitch from Upper Montclair. Couldn't stand losing to a slum girl from Newark."

She gives an exaggerated smile and takes a sip of her 7Up. I cut the sandwich in half and take it out to the bar. When I come back she's standing by the window, looking out at the alley. She turns to me. "I was good, you know. My parents were even gonna send me to one of those gymnastics factories down in Houston. Then things went to hell."

"What happened?"

She sighs. "I'd had enough anyway, but they started threatening to kill each other and I started looking for ways to get out. Started getting high."

"At eleven?"

"Maybe not till twelve. But yeah."

"Jesus." When I was twelve I was still into dinosaurs and baseball cards.

"It wasn't exactly a nurturing environment," Spit says. "Daddy hit us both a lot — just with an open palm, but that was how he controlled me and my mother. What about you?"

"What?"

"You never say anything. About you."

"Oh." I take a cloth and start wiping the steel table that I make the sandwiches on, knocking the crumbs to the floor. "I been here all my life."

"And you don't plan to stay."

"I'll get out next summer."

"To your dad's?"

I start drumming on the table. "Maybe. Doubt it. I think if he wanted me with him he would have waited till I could go." I'm better off without him, just like he and I were better off when my mom left. That doesn't mean I'm doing great, though.

And I don't have any more parents left to shed.

I look hard at Spit, trying to get a sense of her, but she's hard to figure. "Why are *you* here?"

She gives a short, breathy laugh. "Cowardice, I guess. I don't know why else I'd come running back to my mother."

I open the refrigerator and take out a hamburger for myself, tossing it on the grill. "You want anything?" I ask.

She gives a repulsed sort of look, hanging out her tongue. "Not if it's been walking around." She doesn't eat meat. I've never seen her eat much of anything.

"You're no coward," I say.

"Yeah, I am."

"You get up there on the stage and sing for four hours. That takes guts."

She shakes her head. "For you it would," she says. "No, I mean it. It's the most natural thing in the world for me. If I'm not singing, I'm lost."

"Like being on a basketball court for me."

"I guess."

"I wanna do what you do," I say.

"Self-destruct?"

"No. Sing sometime. Rock. Reach my limit."

She laughs. "Join me. Anytime."

"I'm thinking about it." I was dismissed from the school chorus in fifth grade because I "needed practice." I was dismissed *during* practice, which, it seems to me, would be the time to get the practice you need. What the teacher really meant was, "you are beyond help."

"I have no rhythm, no ability to play even the most basic chords on any instrument, and no voice whatsoever," I say.

Spit smiles and nods slowly. "We'll see," she says. "We'll get you up there. It's not all about playing instruments."

I guess I blush. Spit rubs out her cigarette on the table and gets up to leave. I flip the hamburger, turn on the radio, and watch her walk through the doorway.

The county group home is on the corner of Twelfth and Church, a block in from Main Street and just across from the Pocono River, which splits the town in half. It used to be a juvenile prison back in like the '50s, but now it's a group home for the mentally disabled. There's a paved basketball court outside — we call it the Mental Court — and they keep the lights on late, so there's always a crowd of basketball players and other kids standing around smoking.

Tryouts for the high school team are coming up, so the crowd has increased lately. I play there or at the Y any night I'm not working.

Brian Kaipo, who has started at varsity point guard since we were sophomores, usually shows about 9 o'clock and sticks around for a game or two, staying sharp but keeping above the fray. He lives out in Prompton, so he drives into town, parking his parents' car alongside the others in the Episcopal Church lot next door.

This crowd averages younger than the players at the Y, and the game is quicker and cleaner. Guys like Gordie Rickard and Alan Murray can get above the rim, and just about everybody can hit a three-pointer if he's open.

Less than half of these guys will try out for the team, though. A guy like Dave Artuso would never give up his job at the Price-Right supermarket out on Route 6 to play for a guy like Buddy. The money's too good, the coach is a dick, and he can get all the ball he needs right here.

Guys like me and Alan Murray, on the other hand, can't wait for the season to get started. That's why we're out here, wringing sweat from our T-shirts even though it's only fifty degrees out.

Kaipo's another story. He's the only guy on the team with a prayer of playing college ball, even at a Division 3 school like Wilkes or Marywood. He says a few schools have shown interest. But he's on the small side and has to have a kick-ass senior season or he'll be going nowhere.

VISIONS AND REVISIONS

We start slow on these early mornings, but this week it gets pretty intense. We go full-court.

Maybe I'm a better player than Dana, I don't know. I mean, I'm a guy, so I can push with more force, run a little faster. But she's so well-schooled in the basics of the game. Her outside shot is just about perfect in form, and it never varies. She never makes a stupid pass or tries to do too much, like most of the guys I play against.

But what makes her so good is what she does without the ball, the way she sets screens, or moves to the right place on the court, or cuts toward the basket at the exact right instant. This has always been the weakness in my game, knowing what to do when I'm not in the center of the action.

She drives. I've got the lane blocked. She kind of bounces off me and I catch an elbow in the ribs. She dishes off the ball, swings around toward the hoop, and grabs a high, lofting return pass as I steady myself, a hand to her waist. She goes up, fades back, and shoots as my arm smacks her wrist.

The shot misses as we come down parallel, body to body. "You want that?" I say.

"What?"

"The foul."

"No way."

My team gets the rebound. I sprint up to the arc, take the outlet pass, and keep running. They've got one guy back and Dana's right with me, and all of my teammates are behind me. I easily dart past the guy and go hard to the hoop, making the layup over Dana's outstretched hand with her taut, extended body pressing into mine.

"Nice shot," she says.

I jog backwards, staying close to her as we move upcourt. She's quite a specimen.

Quite.

I was supposed to check in with Shorty every day, whether I'm working or not. That arrangement lasted about a week. But Shorty will stick his head into the kitchen from time to time, say something like, "How's it going?" and I'll give a fifteen-second update. This is the extent of the guardianship.

"That toilet working okay?" Shorty says.

"Still gotta jiggle the handle to get it to stop running sometimes, but yeah."

Shorty just smirks and nods. I'm the first full-time resident of room number 3 in years. Before that, it was available, cheap, for a night or an hour at a time. It's said that my father had been an occasional customer.

"Hear from your old man lately?" Shorty asks.

"Called him last weekend," I say. "He sounded okay. Says hi."

Shorty shakes his head. "Los Angeles. Land of losers, smog, and faggots. You wouldn't get me out there for nothing."

What he's implying is: why the hell is my father out there, anyway? Well, what I know is that we were two months behind on the rent, he was about to lose his job managing the day shift at the Sturbridge Inn, and he owed at least a small amount of money right here to Shorty. I'm pretty sure that's just the tip of the iceberg.

What my father says is that it was something he always dreamed of doing, and now was the time. "It's just something I gotta do," he told me when we were packing up the car. "I spent my whole life here and I can't stand it another day. I need warm air. I need culture. I need to meet blondes in bikinis."

"He needs to eat a few."

That's Alan Murray talking to me during an outdoor four-on-four game, full-court. A kid named Ricky, just a sophomore, has been driving the lane effectively, hitting a couple of soft fall-aways from eight feet. "He needs a facial," Alan tells me, letting his emotions charge up just a little. He's not a guy who's going to take shit from anybody.

Next time down, Alan eases off his man when Ricky drives. The kid makes the same move as the last two times, a little pump fake, then rising for the shot. Alan's all over it, smacking it upcourt.

"In your face," he says as he moves past Ricky, adding a little nudge with his shoulder. Alan races upcourt, floats into the key, takes the quick bounce pass from me, and lays it in cleanly. He runs backwards toward the opposite basket, shaking out his arms and nodding vigorously. He's ready for the tryouts.

Tendinitis

Friday night arrives and I don't feel like being here. People keep playing unlucky-at-love songs on the jukebox.

Spit's band comes on about 10:15, a welcome relief from the canned stuff. I tap my fingers with the melody on the edge of the sink. And then I look up, and there's this vision in the doorway. She's about five-foot-six, brownish hair to her shoulders, a little bronze cross on a chain.

"You the guy in charge?" she says.

"In charge of hamburgers." I try to give her a mature smile. "Want one?"

She grins. "Could I get some ice?"

"Yeah. Like in a cup?"

"How about a plastic bag? I've got this tendinitis in my elbow, and it's aching. It'll be fine if I can ice it for five minutes."

"Sure." I take a bag of corn from the freezer and say, "You can sit in here while you ice it, if you want," which is very charitable of me. I suppose she's twenty-one, because Shorty checks I.D.'s, but it can't be by more than a couple of minutes. "What'd you do?"

"It's just tennis elbow," she says. "I played about four hours this afternoon."

"Cold out."

"Indoors."

"Oh. You good?"

"I'm all right. I'll be playing on the team over at the U." The University of Scranton, she means.

She's got the corn on the sandwich table and is leaning over to rest her elbow on it. Another cute woman sticks her head in the kitchen. "Julie?" she says.

"Hi."

"What are you doing?"

"This nice guy is letting me use his kitchen to fix my injury," she says. She points at me. "This is . . ."

"Jay," I say.

"Hello, Jay," the one in the doorway says. "We're gonna dance," she says to this other one with the ice.

The ice girl nods. "Give me two minutes."

Two minutes. Two minutes. "So," I say. "Where . . . uh . . . You like the U?"

"Yeah. Where do you go? Or don't you?"

"Not yet," I say. "I'm like, working for a while first."

"Oh. Well, college is cool."

"I imagine."

She looks around the kitchen, then her eyes rest on me.

"So," I say. "Tennis, huh?"

"Yeah. You play?"

"Not really. I play basketball."

"Good game." She gets up. "Hey, thanks," she says.

"No problem." *Don't leave now.* "I'll put this in the freezer. Come back if you get stiff again . . . Julie."

"Thanks. I think I'll be all right."

"Have fun dancing," I say.

"I will. Have fun making hamburgers."

"I always do."

TRYOUTS

I have no illusions that I will make it to the NBA, or that I'll even play college ball. I just want to wring everything out of this body, take it as far as I'm able. I don't even expect to be a starter this season — we've got the best point guard in the league in Brian Kaipo — but I think I can earn some significant playing time backing him up. First I have to make the team, of course.

There are about forty guys in the gym when I get there, shooting at all six baskets. I pick up a ball and start dribbling, checking out the competition.

Coach blows his whistle, and we all take a seat on the floor. He runs through the procedure: three days of tryouts and he'll take ten guys for varsity; twelve underclassmen will make JV, and two of them will also sit varsity.

Five varsity guys are back from last year, and three of them are guards. So I figure there's maybe two slots I could fill, but probably only one.

51

"Get in groups of six or seven for layups," Coach says. "Bounce passes, nothing fancy. Let's go."

We shoot layups from both sides, then jump shots and free throws. The coaches walk around from group to group, but they already know what most of us can do. After an hour of drills he says to take a three-minute break and we'll scrimmage. He calls six guys over and spends about thirty seconds talking to them. Then those six start walking to the locker room, shaking their heads. Coach didn't waste time making the first cuts. He goes over to Kaipo and a couple of the other returnees.

We get two five-on-five full-court scrimmages going, using the side baskets. I get in the stronger group. Coach puts his five likely starters on the floor and tells me to line up at point guard for the other side. That's a good sign, except that I'll be guarding Kaipo.

Kaipo's maybe five-foot-ten, a couple of inches taller than me. He's got wide-set, pale-blue eyes, and they're crossed just enough to be noticeable. He's a deadly shooter. He hits long-range three-pointers on their first two trips downcourt, but Coach doesn't say anything.

I make a few nice looks inside, hitting

big guys for layups, but our side is getting beat pretty good. Kaipo's scored twice more before I get a hand on a pass, knocking it upcourt and chasing it down. I've got the ball and a full stride on anybody else, and I drive to the hoop and lay the ball gently off the backboard for two.

Coach finally speaks to Kaipo. "Move your ass, Brian," he says. He brings in that blond sophomore, Ricky, for me a few minutes later, nodding to me as I leave the court. I get a drink and sit against the wall.

I go in for Kaipo a while later, getting some minutes with the probable starters. I'm feeling good about this; Coach is giving me a fair shot and I'm playing all right. I cover Ricky, and we're pretty well-matched. He seems tentative, though, scared even. I get a couple of steals, another fast-break layup. He hits a couple of jumpers, makes some decent passes.

I'm good at dishing the ball off, finding the open man, but I have trouble knowing what to do next, where to go. It's an instinct guys like Kaipo were born with, but I'm missing it. I have to keep telling myself what to do instead of it being a natural part of my game.

We run line drills, shoot more free

throws, and hit the locker room. I don't say much of anything, just shower and get dressed. Two more days of this, then he'll pick the team. Based on today, I think I'll make it.

I drink about nine gallons of water, then leave the locker room at ten to 6. That gives me just enough time to check my mail before the post office closes. I average about one worthwhile piece of mail a week, but I look in my box every day anyway. Today there's an envelope: a letter from my father.

They're closing up, so I take it outside to read. There's a check for a hundred bucks. I'll cash it as soon as I can, because it'll probably bounce again. He wants me to call him. He says I need to get a phone. He wants to know what I'm planning to do for Thanksgiving, that it wouldn't kill me to go to my mother's for a day or two.

I look up and Spit's walking toward me.

"Hey," I say.

"Jay. What's going on?"

"Nothing." I fold the letter and stick it in my pocket. "What about you?"

"Nothing," she says. "You're not working?"

"No. You up for anything?"

"Yeah. Anything."

I look around. "Hit the diner?"

"Sure."

We walk the half block up Main Street to the diner and take a seat in a booth.

"I started writing some new songs today," she says.

"At work?"

"Yeah. I had nothing to do, so I typed lyrics into the computer. I'm trying to blend punk with some traditional Portuguese stuff."

The attorney she works for is fresh out of school and doesn't do a lot of business. His father is a prominent real-estate/insurance guy, and he put his soft, nerdy son through law school and set him up in an office above his. Spit does his typing and some research.

"He's such a weenie," she says. "I don't know what he thought I was working on. He's got like two appointments all week. I figure if I look busy he won't get rid of me, but there ain't a whole lot to do."

"You think he'll dump you?"

"Nah. He's too worried about his image. He wouldn't be caught dead answering his own phone. And his father pays my salary anyway. Just till he gets established, he says. Ha."

The waitress — the new one — comes over and asks if we're ready to order. Spit asks for tea with lemon. "And maybe some toast."

I say, "Orange juice. I don't know what else. . . . Soup maybe."

"We have clam chowder and cream of broccoli."

"I guess chowder."

"Cup or a bowl?"

"Um, a bowl." This is dinner. I'll cash the check and eat good tomorrow. "Extra crackers, please."

Spit pushes back her hair. "You make the team?"

"Don't know yet."

"You care?"

"Yeah. I care a lot."

She nods, then keeps nodding and turns it into a kind of dance, back and forth with her shoulders and all. "You need your rushes, too, huh?"

"I don't know. Maybe. I don't think of it like that. It's kind of pure. Just energy. Like you block out everything else and just use what you got."

"Yeah," she says. "Try singing in the spotlight sometime. You might like it."

Each booth has its own little jukebox thing. You turn a silver wheel on top to flip through the selections. She starts going through it, saying, "Lame. Lame. Decent. Lame. . . . You got any quarters?"

I check. "I've got one."

"Good enough." She takes it and punches in some numbers.

"You like *this?*" I say when Frank Sinatra comes on, singing "Let Me Try Again."

"It's honest," she says. "Yeah, I like it." She kicks me gently under the table.

"It looks like it's between me and this sophomore for the last guard spot," I say.

"You should be better than a sophomore, aren't you?"

"Probably. Yeah. But not much. And see, he can start JV and play some varsity, which I can't do because I'm a senior. Plus he's got potential for the next two years."

The waitress brings the soup and the tea and a whole basket of crackers and rolls. She's what, nineteen maybe, with blondish hair pulled back in a ponytail. I thank her warmly and she leaves.

Spit wipes her nose with her hand. "Getting a cold," she says. "So you think you'll get cut?"

"I don't know. It's close. If I play my ass off the rest of the week, I think he'll have to keep me." I stare into space for a few seconds, then shrug. "It ain't up to me."

★ ★ ★

Second day. Kaipo's bringing the ball up slowly and deliberately, grabbing a breath while he can. I pull the front of my T-shirt out of my shorts and wipe the sweat from my face, but it doesn't halt the tide. I'm dripping and panting but I'm into this, it's been intense. You lay off this guy for a second and he kills you, taking advantage of any hesitation. I love it. He kicks my ass most days, but once in a while I have the edge. On those days I know I'm a player, because Kaipo's game never wavers much. If you nail Kaipo twice a year, you remember it.

He crosses midcourt and I shadow him, not quite pressing. We've been guarding each other for half an hour steady and he hasn't outplayed me by much. Coach sent some more guys packing a while ago, so there's only twenty-six left. I know I'm getting a long look because I'm one of the guys who could be sacrificed.

I love the rhythms of basketball, the ups and downs. You get burned a few times, make an awful pass, clank a few shots off the rim. But then you get in harmony, hit two, three jumpers, quick, sharp, like hammering nails.

Kaipo tries to penetrate and I swipe at

the ball. But he gives a quick fake and he's past me, setting up at the top of the key and firing. It swishes.

I take the inbounds pass and dribble up quickly. Kaipo picks me up, focusing hard with those crossed eyes. I pass to Alan Murray on the wing, then take it back. I give a look inside but there's no one open. Murray sets a pick for me at the foul line and I take it and shoot. It swishes, too, and I forget about getting burned on defense.

"Lazy," Coach says to Kaipo. "Fight through those screens, Brian."

Kaipo doesn't acknowledge the coach. He says "nice move" even as Coach is riding him. He dribbles upcourt, drives into the lane, then throws a wild, behind-the-back pass out of bounds.

Coach blows his whistle. He stares hard at Kaipo. "Ricky," he says. "Get in there for Brian."

The guy with the roses usually comes in around 11, walks from one end of the bar to the other, and sells about three flowers a week. It works like this: maybe there's two or three women down one end, kind of huddled together in a cloud of cigarette smoke. Some factory-working cowboy or a plumber's assistant will hand the flower guy three bucks, point out the woman he thinks is most vulnerable, and send the guy over to her with a paid-for rose. I've seen this happen enough times to know that it doesn't work.

I've thought about it, though. This week especially, like if Julie ever comes back with her tennis elbow and interested smile. Maybe that could work.

Or maybe I could get the guy to walk into the gym some Tuesday morning at 6. Ha.

Third day. Kaipo and two of the other starters are sitting on the stairs to the gym when I leave the locker room. He nods as I come up.

"Jay," he says.

"Hi."

"Cut day," he says.

"Right." I stop two steps below him and shrug.

"You should make it," he says.

"You think?"

"I do, yeah." He looks around. "That doesn't mean it'll happen."

I take a seat. I like Brian, but we haven't ever been close. He's started varsity since our sophomore year, when I was just barely playing JV.

He leans in close and squints. "He's big on this kid Ricky, if you haven't noticed."

"Yeah. I noticed." I also know that I've been outplaying Ricky all week, even if only by a little.

"Coach isn't real objective," Kaipo says. "You better kick ass today."

I put out a palm and he slaps it. He's a decent man with big hands. "Thanks," I say. I get up and go to the gym.

Coach explains that he's already notified ten kids that they'll be playing JV this season, and he's sent them home. He cut two others after yesterday's workout, so that leaves fourteen of us warming up for today's session, dribbling basketballs and stretching.

I compute the problem while we go through our passing and shooting drills. Twelve of the fourteen guys left are going to stick, and two of them will be under-classmen who'll play JV and sit varsity. There are eight seniors here. You have to figure that the six remaining under-classmen are considered better than the ten he already picked for JV, so it's a guar-antee that the two players cut will be seniors.

I swallow hard. This doesn't look good.

It looks worse when he lines Ricky up at point guard against Kaipo at the start of the scrimmage. I take a seat on the bleachers and rest my chin on my thumbs.

Alan Murray, who is half-black, with very short hair and big shoulders, sits next to me. I turn to him and we both give a smirk of recognition. He's a senior, too, about six-foot-three, and he's got good court instincts but unreliable hands. He has the same look of impending doom that I think is all over my face.

I get in after about fifteen minutes, taking Kaipo's spot opposite Ricky. He's been playing with more confidence today. It's obvious that he'll at least be starting JV, so the pressure's off him and it shows. He beat Kaipo a couple of times, made some good passes inside, and just seems a lot looser overall.

Murray comes in, too, playing forward for my side. If I look for him, he'll probably look for me.

I make a sloppy pass right away, and Ricky takes it and runs. I catch up and edge him away from the basket, but he fires a no-look pass to Monahan coming down the lane and he lays it in cleanly.

Okay. I'm cold, he's warm. But one play

doesn't mean much.

I dribble up the court and we move the ball around, looking for a pass inside. I'll keep the tempo slow until I've been up and down the court a few times, until I get in a groove.

The pass comes to me at the top of the key, and Ricky stays in his stance, daring me to shoot the three-pointer. I take the dare but the ball just grazes the rim. Our center grabs the rebound and lays it in.

Next time up I don't hesitate. I make a quick pass to Murray and immediately yell for the ball back. He passes it to me in the same spot and I take the jumper, hitting it.

Ricky covers me closer next time. I drive into the lane and pop it out to Murray, who hits the fifteen-footer. We slap hands as we run back on defense.

It's back and forth like that for half an hour, until Coach puts Kaipo back in for me.

I did what I can do. I watch the rest of the scrimmage, run the line drills, shoot my twenty free throws, and take a good look around the gym before heading down the stairs.

I sit on the bench by my locker and wipe my face with a towel. I held my own today,

I played even with Ricky. But I know that wasn't enough.

Coach is walking through the locker room. He comes to me and puts his hand on my shoulder. "Come on in a minute," he says.

I close my eyes. Shit. I nod and go to his office. He doesn't follow.

When he comes in, he's got Alan Murray with him. Coach leans against his desk and folds his arms. "This is the toughest part of being a coach," he says.

Alan's looking at the floor. I bite my lip but keep my eyes on the coach.

"I don't mind cutting guys who don't deserve to be here," he says. "Guys who don't hustle or come in out of shape or have a crummy attitude." He lets out a sigh. "It's tougher with guys like you."

We don't say anything. I knew this was coming, but I'm stunned anyway.

"I've decided to go with a younger lineup this year," he says. "Thanks for giving it your all."

I forgive the clichés because you can tell he means it. But this sucks. I can't believe it's over.

"There's a new league starting at the Y," Coach says. "Just for high school kids. The churches are sponsoring the teams. I know it's not the same, but you can still play ball if you want. I hope you will."

It's not the same all right. Not by a long shot.

Coach says, "What church do you go to, Alan?"

Alan says he's a Methodist.

"They'll have a team," Coach says. "Talk to your minister." He looks at me. "How about you?"

"Uh, Methodist," I say. I went to the Methodist preschool for a year, but I haven't been near a church since. Alan gives me a puzzled look. I think he actually goes.

Coach shakes our hands and we leave his office. I go to my locker and get changed in a hurry. Alan sits on the end of the bench, facing the wall, still in his sweaty shorts and T-shirt.

I need to get out of here. Alan's crying. I just want to go home and lie down.

Early evening there's a knock at my door. I get off the mattress and check it out. Spit's standing there in a maroon down vest.

"Thought you'd be working tonight," she says.

"Not until Friday." I wave her in and

shut the door. She sits on the radiator, so I take the chair.

"What's going on?" she asks.

I just shake my head.

"Got cut, huh?"

"How'd you know?"

"You just look it." She slaps her palms on her thighs. "Wanna get drunk?"

I look at her face for three seconds, then look down. "Nah."

She stands up and crosses her arms. "I do."

I shrug.

"You been staring at the ceiling again, bud?"

I smirk, just slightly. "Some."

"No good," she says. "Come on. Humor me. Let's get out of here."

"I guess." I get my jacket.

We head out and walk through the alley to Main Street. It's getting cold and it's windy, but the air feels good in my lungs. I realize that I'm hungry. Starving.

"Wanna get pizza?" I ask.

"Sure."

Foley's Pizza is next to Shorty's, and it's a good place to kill an hour. We take the first booth so we can look out at the street, and I go up to the counter and get a couple of slices.

Spit puts salt on hers, which seems a little excessive.

"God, what a boring day," she says.

"Yeah?"

"We had zero appointments. Zero phone calls. I actually sat there reading Stanley's Seton Hall alumni magazine. He was out for like three hours getting supplies, which he does about twice a week. We've got enough toilet paper and yellow legal pads until he retires, I think."

She's looking right at me, but I'm mostly looking out at the street. I make eye contact a few times to let her know I'm listening. "He's making me work next Friday," she says. "Day after Thanksgiving, nothing to do, and I've gotta sit there all day in case the phone rings. Plus I feel like shit. Clogged sinuses and all."

"It's going around," I say.

She blows her nose in a napkin and then takes a bite of her pizza, chewing it slowly.

"Want another one?" I say.

"I guess. Yeah."

I get up and get us two more slices.

When I come back, she scrunches up her face to make me laugh. It works, to a degree.

"So," she says. "The dream is over?"

I shrug. "There was no dream."

"But you care."

"I care a lot."

"You angry?"

"No."

"Right. So what are you going to do?" she asks.

"Nothing. What *can* I do?"

"I don't know. Something. I try to take all the shit I've been through and turn it into music. But there's too much left over, so I get high."

"Yeah, well, where do I get my fixes now?" I say. "I mean, all the basketball I've played in the past few months was directed toward making the team. Sunday mornings at the Y just isn't going to cut it."

"You gotta find a way to use that passion," she says. "You gotta let it out. Otherwise some night when you're cold and alone it'll come banging on your door. And it won't be smiling."

"You know about that, huh?"

"All too well, bud." She picks up a pepper shaker and starts turning it over in her hand. She's more introspective tonight than I've ever seen her, which means she's being quiet for fifteen, twenty seconds at a time. "But whatever I do to myself I keep bouncing back from."

I dwell on that a minute. She reaches

over and taps my hand once with her fingers. "For a year I spent all my energy trying to make somebody else happy," she says. "And there was no way. James is brilliant, but he's burdened, and he's too focused inward to let any light out."

"How the hell did you wind up with him anyway?"

"I don't know. But I still miss him. As destructive as that was."

"You miss banging your head against the wall?"

"I guess I do."

"Maybe that's where I come in."

Her eyes get wide and she opens her mouth, laughs a little. "Maybe. Hey, I create or I destroy, you know that." She shakes her head. "Yeah, I wanna make somebody happy. Maybe you. I guess I need that."

I feel a little better suddenly.

"You're a good guy, Jay."

I nod slowly. "Yeah. Whatever that means."

And then we're quiet for a while, looking out the window. They've got the oldies station playing in here, and the Supremes come on. "My father's favorite group," she says.

"Really?"

"Yeah. He always listens to stuff like this, and the Temptations and the Beatles. And Springsteen's old songs." She really brightens all of a sudden, a broad smile and wider eyes. "Man, we'd drive to the shore sometimes, in the dead of winter even. They'd sing all the way down the Parkway, my parents, and we'd sit on the boardwalk, out of the wind, and think about summer. This is when I was little. We'd make castles out of snow and sand, freezing our asses off, then get coffee and french fries from McDonald's."

"Wow," I say, and I feel happier, too, seeing her that way suddenly. But I don't have memories like that. Not that I can remember.

"My father loves this stuff," she says, and she bites her lip and grins right at me. "I know all the songs, man. Big part of my life. The good part."

"But it didn't last?" I hate to ask that, because it may bring her down, but part of me likes to hear about parents crashing. That's something I can compare to my own life.

"Part of it lasted," she says. "We still have that connection. But my father has too many frustrations, being the low man at work and all, and he never learned how to deal with it. So he'd get drunk and smack my mother. Not all the time. But enough."

She reaches across and slides her hand against mine, so some of the fingertips are touching. The warmth goes up my arms. "And you?" she says.

"What?"

"You know. Where the hell do your parents get off abandoning you?"

I shake my head. "It ain't like that."

"Oh, no?"

I let out a major exhale. "Nah. I don't know. From what I can piece together — you hear this shit from both of them, never straight, just bitching about the other one, but you gotta figure there's some truth in it, right? They got married right out of high school and they're both drinking all the time and taking risks. She's doing drugs, he's screwing around with other women, there's lots of arguments over everything. Some days it's great, but it's never realistic. I come along. We move all the time; they screw the landlords out of rent; they can't hold jobs. My father gets big ideas about the lottery and starts going to Atlantic City and betting at Shorty's on football and basketball and anything. Sometimes he wins big, but . . . you know.

She gets the hell out of here when she can't take it anymore. But she's got a kid, right? You just take off? Like my father's going to just straighten up and take care of me?"

"He did, though."

I nod and look away. "Yeah. He did an okay job. He tried, I'll give him that much. Screw it. It's behind me. I'm living for now, man. I'm over it."

TWO

SALT

I avoided basketball at all costs for a week, but I can't stay away forever. So I do the 5:30 wake-up thing again and get my butt over to the Y.

There are ten of us this time, so we go full-court. I line up opposite Dana and say hello. We nodded to each other in school the other day, and I guess that's part of the reason I'm here at this ridiculous hour.

"You ready to run?" she says.

"Sure."

She starts kind of strolling toward the foul line as play begins, and I shadow her. Then she makes the big cut, curving under the basket as I run straight into a pick set by her father. She's wide open as the pass comes and she swishes the shot from ten feet out.

I take the inbounds pass and turn, and Dana's right in my face. I dribble hard to midcourt, then pass off and drift inside.

"Somebody's ready to go," I say to her.

"I've been here since five-thirty," she

says. "I'm warm."

I'll bet she is. The ball comes to me; I turn my back to her and push toward the basket. She sticks tight to me, gives a little bump. I could shoot, but I kick it out to the corner where one of our guys is open. He shoots an air ball and we lose possession. I chase Dana back upcourt.

By 7 o'clock guys start leaving, and by 7:15 there are only a few of us left, so the game breaks up. I've still got an hour to shower and get to school, so I decide to shoot some free throws.

After a few minutes Dana comes back on the court and rebounds for me.

"So how come you're not playing for the school?" I say.

She shrugs. "Too busy. You?"

"I got cut."

"Too bad."

"It sucks," I say. "They could use you." Hell, the *boys'* team could use her.

"Maybe," she says. "I can't. I played my first three years, but I'm concentrating on jumping this winter, so I really don't have time."

"What do you mean?"

"I'm a high jumper. My college coach wants me to focus on that."

"You have a college coach?"

"I got a full ride to jump at Virginia next year. So it seemed like a good idea to quit basketball. Except for this. Plus we were moving anyway, since my dad took a job up here."

"You must be good."

She raises her eyebrows a little, shifts her shoulders. "I choke in big meets," she says. "I jumped five-eleven last spring, then couldn't even clear five-ten in the states. I finished third. No way that's gonna happen again."

"You gonna jump for Sturbridge this spring?"

"Sure. But my dad will coach me, unofficially. He still jumps, too. In master's meets. He made All American at UVA, so that's why I'm headed there."

"Where do you jump?"

"My dad drives me down to Lehigh two nights a week. See, we're from Allentown, so we know everybody down there. So I jump twice a week and sometimes compete on the weekends. Plus lifting and running. I'll be ready this spring."

Awesome. Her father comes into the gym, fully dressed now, and calls to her. "We'd better get moving, honey."

"Okay." She slaps the ball to me. "See ya, Jay."

"Yeah."

I shoot a few more free throws, but I can't concentrate. That girl is light-years ahead of me.

Thanksgiving is the first major holiday I've ever spent alone. I sleep late, eat a bowl of Cheerios, listen to a couple of tapes, read *Sports Illustrated*, stare at the ceiling.

Shorty won't open until 3 today, so I go downstairs to the bar around noon and put on a football game. I look at the phone a few times; I have to call my father. Later, though.

I go back upstairs at 2:30, eat another bowl of Cheerios, listen to another tape, read the sports section of yesterday's newspaper, stare at the ceiling again. Spit asked me to come over, but I told her I had to work. It isn't true, of course.

I put on my hiking boots, a pair of cotton work gloves, a heavy sweatshirt and a windbreaker, go down the back stairs, and walk through the alley up to Main Street.

I walk along Main, which is empty of people and traffic. I walk the four blocks to the river against a stiff wind, then cross over to Park Street and head toward the cliff. I pass the YMCA and cross the bridge over the creek, then follow a short dirt path until it starts to climb. You have to use your hands here for a few feet, pulling yourself up with roots and hand-holds. Then you're on a real path that circles through the woods, up the hill, toward the cliff that overlooks the town.

I turn off onto another path about three-quarters of the way up, following a ridge that heads into deeper woods. The maple leaves are long fallen, curled brown and frozen underfoot. There are tiny flakes of snow coming down, just on the snow side of frozen rain. The wind is icy. It feels like winter.

"You should have gone down to New Jersey." He sounds disappointed, but con-cerned. My father.

"I had no way to get there."

"Oh, come on. She would have driven up. You know that."

"I didn't feel like it."

"Please call her."

"I will."

"I mean now. As soon as you hang up with me."

"Yeah."

There's a long silence. I'm in the tiny hallway between the bathrooms at the diner, standing next to the pay phone.

"Jay."

"Dad."

"You want to come out here?"

"No." I don't say it as strongly as I feel it. "Not really."

"You can come now. Finish school out here."

"Screw that."

"You're still coming when you graduate?"

"If I graduate."

"What do you mean, if?"

"I don't know. I don't think school's the place for me anymore. I got cut from the basketball team."

"So you want to quit school because of basketball?"

"Not just that."

I hear him take a big breath and an exhale. "Listen. This isn't the best time to talk about all this. You're upset because you got cut and you're alone on a day that we've always been together. Things will be looking better by the weekend, I'm sure."

He's probably right. "I know," I say.

"They will. Now call your mom. Call collect. And call me back in a couple of days. Okay?"

"Yeah."

"I love you, kid."

"I know."

"Keep your chin up."

"See ya."

I hang up. The diner is virtually empty — who eats at a diner on Thanksgiving? But I'm starving and I don't feel like having Cheerios again. So I take a booth.

There are two old burnouts way down the end of the counter drinking coffee, a guy about my father's age at the register, and the new waitress. We're the only people in here.

The waitress smiles at me and comes over with a questioning kind of look on her face. "Hi," she says. Her name tag says Brenda.

"Hey."

"Just you?" she says.

"Uh, yeah. Just need a quick bite."

"Oh. You need a menu?"

"Nah."

"Okay. Well we have turkey and stuff. Maybe you already had enough of that today?"

I smile and nod, lying with my gestures. "I think I'll get chicken salad on a roll. With, um, fries and a Coke."

"Sure. You want cranberry sauce? We're giving it away."

"Nah. Maybe a salad, though."

"Okay."

She comes back two minutes later with the Coke and a big bowl of salad. There's extra things in it like raw broccoli and carrot sticks. The waitress is wearing a white T-shirt and black jeans, and her ponytail is starting to unravel.

"The sandwich'll be ready in a minute," she says.

"Thanks."

She walks away nicely and I feel the kind of pang I've been getting a lot of lately.

After she brings the sandwich, she goes to the end of the counter to check on the coffee guys, then comes back down to my end and sits at a booth in the corner. There are about twenty small clear salt shakers on the table, and she starts filling them from one of those big cylindrical containers, leaning way over so she doesn't spill any. She's more or less on the periphery of my vision, so I can watch her without being obvious. When I glance up, the guy at the register is giving me a look. Maybe that's her father, I don't know. But he doesn't like the way I'm looking at her, and he's probably right about that.

I ought to tell her that I work at Shorty's. Maybe she'll come by. Spit's playing tomorrow night; it would be fun, even though I'll be working.

She comes over and asks if everything's all right. I say it's great. "You're new, huh?" I say.

"Yeah. We just moved here. So I'm stuck working the holiday."

"I know the feeling."

"You too?"

"Not today. But all weekend. Over there," I say, pointing across the street. "At Shorty's."

"What is that, a bar?"

"Yeah. Good place."

"You tend bar?"

"Uh, no. I cook."

"Oh. That's what my boyfriend does. He made that sandwich."

Shit. "Oh," I say. "He works here?"

"Yeah. We both do."

So much for that idea.

"I'll get your check," she says. "Unless you want some dessert or something."

"No. I gotta get out of here. But thank you."

"All righty."

Sprawling on a Pin

Friday night Spit comes in during a break. Shorty lets her keep wine and beer for the band in here so they don't have to go up to the bar. She takes a wine bottle out of the refrigerator and pours a big glassful.

"What's up?" she says.

"Not much. Good crowd."

"Definitely." She reaches into her pocket and takes a fat white pill out of a prescription bottle. "I still got that crappy throat from this cold," she says.

"What'd you do, go to a doctor?"

"No. I found these in my mother's medicine cabinet."

"Oh."

"I better take two," she says. "This cold sucks." She chases them down with half the glass of wine and wipes her mouth. She punches her chest with a fist, her bracelets bouncing on her bare arm. "Righteous," she says. She shakes her head and gives me a goofy smile.

★ ★ ★

I keep getting visitors. Bo sticks his head in around midnight and gives me that faintly theatrical look, wide-eyed, like he freezes for a second, expressing mock surprise at finding me here. That's how he greets everybody.

Bo's maybe twenty-two, but he's a comfortable regular. He's small, with long curly hair and a little blond beard. He's always wearing a Harley-Davidson painter's cap, and he's an expert with a cigarette. Everybody likes him, the way he nurses a beer. Even the old guys who've been coming here forever and won't change their routines for nothing. They're out there tonight, on their regular stools. They don't care if Spit's on and it's wall-to-wall kids, or it's a weeknight with the TV and three other old guys.

"Bo," I say.

He nods. "Keeping busy?"

"Not too right now," I say. "What's going on out there?"

"Take a look."

I come to the door. It's the regular scene. At least the regular scene when Spit's group is playing. Lots of denim and bare navels. Navels and those little green bottles of Rolling Rock seem to go together. Along with Marlboro Lights, I'm afraid.

I clean up the kitchen about 1 o'clock because there's not likely to be more orders. The band is still on when I finish, so I lean against the doorframe to catch the end of the set. The room is still pretty full; a few girls are dancing, and a few couples. The frenzy level is high, and the noise, but Spit is gyrating very slowly, eyes closed, furiously singing "Ironbound" in the bright white light:

> *I walk these streets like litter*
> *I walk these streets like rain*
> *He talks, he cheats, he hit her*
> *He makes me share her pain*

Julie the elbow-icer is one of the ones on the floor, dancing with her girlfriends. I melt a little more. A scruffy guy in a loose flannel shirt with brown and black squares moves over and motions something like "you want to dance?" She grins and shifts her attention toward him. They dance until the song ends, then he asks if he can buy her a drink. She smiles and says, "no thanks." He gives a sheepish smile and goes back to the bar. Another song starts and one of Julie's girlfriends comes over to her. I see her raise her eyebrows and they laugh and start dancing again.

I'm the boy who washes dishes, who's not even supposed to be out here. But I'm watching her dance and it's like I'm an arm's length from cracking this, an arm's length that might as well be a light-year.

I go out in the alley, look up at the moon. It's one of those clear, cold nights, and though the bar is noisy you can step out into the lot and be right in your own quiet space.

The church league. I guess that has to be my answer. No sense giving it up now. The cold air feels right against my face, here in this corner of the evening.

Spit's in the kitchen when I go back, leaning against the table. "Thirsty as hell," she says. She takes another dose of the antibiotic and chugs another glass of wine. "You okay, bud? You look, I don't know . . . odd."

"Nah. Just regular."

She yawns. "Yeah?"

"Yeah. But regular sucks."

"You know better," she says. "Goofy optimism, remember?"

I rub my hands together. I'm not so down, really. "Just reflecting on life," I say, trying to sound ironic.

"Life. Yeah." She climbs up on the table to sit. "Purge it, man. Force the moment to its crisis."

I give her what feels like a blank stare.

"Eliot," she explains. "The real one. Go."

I feel myself blush. She's different tonight. Way wired. "Frustration. You know, sexually."

"Hey," she says, "tough it out. The human body can endure."

"Yeah? Like forever?"

She shrugs. "No biggie, bud. I haven't had sex in almost a year and I'm all right."

I smirk. I don't like her this way.

"Well," she says, "that's not entirely true."

"No?"

"Not if you count this afternoon."

"Today?"

She takes another swig of wine, this time from the bottle. "Well, it barely registered. But yeah."

I'm wondering who this could have been with. A guy in the band, maybe? But she worked all day.

"We had nothing to do, so he calls me into the office and asks if I want to smoke some grass with him."

Oh, shit. "You went to bed with the lawyer?"

"A couch." She laughs. "He had really good grass. I hadn't been high in a long time, so I said what the hell. Then, you know. Whatever."

Whatever. "The fat lawyer?"

"It was just recreational." She giggles. "It's pretty hilarious until you think about it."

I shake my head.

"Why do you care?" She says it with a smile, but with a bit of a challenge, like she's testing whether I'm jealous. She puts her arm across my shoulder. "Come on, let's crash," she says. "The room is spinning and I'm beat."

I wake up to the soft sound of gagging and find Spit all hunched up, puking on my bed. I lurch away and turn on the light, checking myself for vomit. "Spit?" I say.

Her skin is very pale and there are tiny drops of sweat all over her face. She's still got her eyes closed and she doesn't answer right away. Then she groans. "My stomach is killing me," she says.

The puke looks bloody and I turn away fast.

"I'm dying," she says.

"You are?"

"Oh, shit. No. But I ought to. Oh, shit."

I don't know what to do. It's 4 o'clock in the morning. I look around the room, out the window.

"Get an ambulance."

"Really?"

"Really. Oh, shit. Go on."

I run downstairs to the bar and dial 911. I tell them the situation and they say they'll get right over. I'm not sure if I should go upstairs or wait by the back door till they get here. Son of a bitch. I go back upstairs.

She's throwing up again when I get there. "They're coming," I say. I go into the bathroom and wet a washcloth. I wring it out and put in on the back of her neck. I really don't know why.

She manages to say thanks. I go outside and the ambulance pulls in about three minutes later, lights flashing but no siren. Two paramedics get out and I point to the stairs.

They go up and one of them takes her pulse.

"You the boyfriend?" the other one says.

I shake my head. "No. Just a friend, man. She was just crashing here tonight."

"What's her name?"

"Spit . . . Sarita."

"What does she have in her?"

"A lot of wine, I guess."

"Any drugs?"

"I don't know." I never know with Spit. "She was taking some cold medicine. A prescription. It's in her shirt pocket." I look for the shirt. "Over there."

He frowns. "Anything else?"

"I really don't know. It's possible. She was smoking grass this afternoon."

"Okay," he says. "She have parents?"

"A mother."

"You better call her."

"I don't know her."

"Oh."

They start talking to Spit. She's not exactly coherent.

"We'll take her in," one guy says. He looks around the room. "You better come along."

I sit in the waiting room for at least an hour, but they aren't telling me shit. They said she'll be all right; that's about all.

I've been nodding on and off in a chair, wishing I'd brushed my teeth. I look up and there's a heavier, older, more conservative version of Spit by the desk. It has to be her mother.

She comes over and takes a seat, smiling at me.

I smile back. She seems pleasant. Kind of pretty for her age and the time of day. "You Spit's mother?" I say.

"Yes. I'm going in to see her in a moment." The mother does have an accent. New Jersey Hispanic.

"They said she'll be okay," I say.

"Yes. This time. But this isn't the first time. And probably not the last." She squints a little and looks me up and down. "And who might you be?" she asks.

"Oh. I'm Jay. I work at the bar. Where her band was."

"Ah," she says. "And you are not having your stomach pumped this evening?"

I smile, hold back a laugh. "No. I don't indulge."

"You're wise," she tells me. "Wiser than Sarita, I see."

I tilt my head. "I don't know about that."

She raises her eyebrows, then stands up. "I'll go and see her now. Perhaps you should, too."

"I don't think they'll let me."

"*I'll* let you. Come along."

We walk to the emergency room and I punch a square red button to open the doors. Then I push another square red button to open another set.

92

There's a guy sitting on a bench with blood on his shirt and his right hand wrapped in gauze. We walk past him and look into an empty room, then walk to the next one.

Spit's lying on a bed in there with an I.V. tube in her arm. "Hi, Mom," she says weakly. She stretches out my name. "Jay."

"You're alive," I say.

She laughs. "Yeah. But that eternal footman was leering at me big-time."

Her mother puts her hand on Spit's forehead and frowns. "Oh, daughter," she says.

"Oh, Mommy."

I let out a sigh of relief, but suddenly I feel like I'm intruding. I give Spit a little wave. I catch her mother's eye and say good night.

They both say good-bye. Her mother says thank you.

I leave through the sets of double doors and I can't wait to get home and back to sleep. But then I remember what my bed looks like and imagine how the room smells. I look up at the clock; it's 5:37. I rub my eyes. I guess I'll go get breakfast.

I have to wait fifteen minutes for the diner to open, so I sit on the steps with my eyes closed. At about five of, a waitress opens the door. I look up and she smiles at me.

"Going fishing?" she asks, like she's making a joke.

"No." I turn my head toward her. "Just had an unusual night."

I know this woman, sort of, because I have breakfast here a couple of days a week. She's kind of like you'd expect a morning waitress at a diner would be, sort of motherly.

"Come on in," she says.

I sit in a booth even though I'm alone, because it's a hell of a lot more comfortable than the counter. I rub my eyes with my fists.

"Do you know what you want, honey?" the waitress asks.

"I guess pancakes. With fried ham and orange juice. A huge orange juice."

I figure I'll ball up the sheets and dump them in the sink for now, drag the mattress out into the hall, prop the window open with a brick, spray deodorant around the room, put on a warm sweat suit, climb into my sleeping bag, and stretch out on the floor. I'll do laundry this afternoon. I can deal with all this. But only after I get some sleep.

Nine-and-a-Half

My mother left home the same evening I got hit in the chest with an orange she'd flung across the kitchen. I didn't get hurt, and the orange had been aimed at my father, but she left in tears anyway, saying she was no good for me.

I was nine and I didn't agree, but I see it clearer now. She was a drunk and she hated my father, who she accused of sleeping with every warm body he could get into. The funny thing is, in the eight years that he and I lived alone together, he never slept with anyone that I know of.

The orange didn't hurt, like I said, and I don't think the verbal assaults did either. "You're just like your father" has always been her most frequent statement to me, though in what way I was like him was never made clear. I think it's her way of praying that I *don't* turn out like him. I suppose that's the best she can do for me.

Monday. I take a tray and push it along

95

the lunch line, looking around the cafeteria for Alan Murray. I don't see him. The two girls in front of me are giggling, talking back and forth. One's short and the other's tall, but they're both slender and they've got tight faded jeans on and attitudes that make it clear this school is just water off their backs. "So I went out with him," the shorter one is saying, "but, like, just to make Kurt jealous."

The taller one turns and looks my way. I meet her eyes but I don't hold them.

I take a hoagie and a chocolate milk and get out of line. And I see Alan over in a corner, sitting with two black guys. If you count Alan, there are nine-and-a-half black guys in the whole school. One of the guys with him is Jared Hall, who starts at forward. The other one is Anthony something, and he doesn't play sports that I know of.

I go over anyway. I set down my tray and they look up. "Anybody here?" I say, mostly looking at Alan.

"No," he says. "Sit down."

I nod to Jared, who's sitting across from me.

"Tough break getting cut," he says.

"Yeah. It sucks."

Alan looks at me, nods.

"That's what I wanted to talk to you about," I say.

"What?"

"What do you know about this church league? I mean, can I get on your team?"

"Maybe," Alan says. "We got like seven guys now."

"Six," says Anthony.

Alan turns to look at him. "You bailing?"

"I was only going to play so you'd have enough," Anthony says. "Take this man instead."

"Yeah, take me. But keep him, too," I say, pointing to Anthony.

"Well," Alan says, "you're supposed to be in our youth group to play."

"So sign me up."

Alan rubs his jaw. "You start coming to meetings?"

"I guess. Yeah."

"I mean, I'd like you to play," he says. "You're a good player and all. But I do care about the youth group. I mean, some people think it's a joke." He takes a sip of his Sprite. "I don't."

Anthony looks around at me from the other side of Alan. "He's president," he says.

Okay, so there's a condition attached to my being in the church league. I actually have to hook up with a church. Fair enough.

"So when do you meet?" I ask.

"We meet Sundays at six," he says. "This week we meet at the Y. For practice."

I smile. "I can handle that."

Alan fixes his eyes on me. "Services are at eleven," he says. "Maybe I'll see you there."

We play half-court on Tuesday morning, which is more a test of skill for me than my full-court running game. But I play well; it feels good to be back. Later I ask Dana how the jumping's going.

"Hit a snag," she says. "We were looking at tapes and decided that I'm not going to go much higher unless I try a new approach. A variation on what I've been doing. So it's like back to square one." She pulls up her tank top to wipe the sweat from her face, revealing her tight abdominal muscles.

"So now I'm struggling to clear five-six," she says, "but once I nail the new form I'll be going higher than I ever would have before."

"Is that frustrating?"

"A little," she says. "I find myself lapsing into the old style just to get over the bar sometimes. But I fight it. I know I have to regress a little in order to get better."

Spit doesn't come around until Wednesday, but she seems like her old self. She rushes into the kitchen.

"We got another gig," she says.

"Where?"

"Ground Zero. Over in Weston." She does a comical little dance, like the twist. "I'm psyched."

"When?"

"Friday. This Friday. Somebody backed out and they called us."

"You ain't playing here?"

"Not this week. No. We weren't supposed to. Shorty's bringing in a DJ on Friday and some other band on Saturday."

"So you're moving up in the world."

"Nah. We'll be back here next week. But this is cool, isn't it? We never played anywhere else."

"Wow, what's next? Scranton?"

She laughs. "Oh, jeez, that'd be like too much to even think about. I mean *Scranton.*"

I give her a high five. She's beaming. I notice that her eyes are sort of bloodshot.

"What's with the eyes?" I ask.

"Nothing. Remember last weekend when

my body was rejecting my stomach? I broke some blood vessels from barfing so hard. No big deal."

"You kind of overdid it."

"It was just that medicine," she says. "I think I was allergic to it."

I roll my eyes. "Maybe it was the thirty glasses of wine."

"Whatever. No big deal."

I fold my arms and squint at her. I'm not about to lecture, but I can't believe she's blowing this off. "Do you say this stuff just to bust my chops?" I ask.

She sticks out her tongue. "Hey, it's happened before," she says. "I just don't make a big thing out of it. I like having fun. What's wrong with that?"

So Friday's looking bleak, with Spit over in Weston crawling toward the big time, and a DJ here cranking out Chuck Berry and Beach Boys songs. I hang in the kitchen all night, but it's slow and boring.

Around midnight I start wiping everything down, shining the counters and the refrigerator and the stovetop.

Somebody says hi from the doorway.

I turn and it's Julie, the tennis player. She's got a Red Barons baseball cap on with a ponytail hanging out the back. I say hi in return, drawing it out to almost two syllables, expressing surprise and delight and interest.

"How's it going?" she asks.

"Uh, well, fine. You been out there all night?"

"No. Just a few minutes. Thought I'd say hello."

She can't mean that she came here just to say hello to me. She must mean that she was here anyway, and, since she was here, she thought she'd check in.

I set the washrag on the table. "You, uh . . . who you with?"

"Those same girls. We were at another bar most of the night."

"Oh. Well, I been here all night."

She laughs, which means she knows I was trying to be funny, even though what I said really wasn't. "I figured."

"Yeah, I'm kind of chained to the stove here. I mean, you know, not all the time."

She looks me up and down, quickly, just a flick of her eyes. "What was your name again?" she says.

"Jay. Same as before. How's your elbow?"

She points it at me. "Not bad. It comes and goes."

"It's beautiful."

She frowns a little, unflexes her arm. The same girl who interrupted last time comes into the doorway. She looks at me, then at Julie, then back at me. She shakes her head. "You coming out?" she says to Julie.

Julie nods. "In a minute."

"Those guys followed us here."

"I figured they would."

Suddenly I feel cut off from the conversation. "What guys?" I ask.

"Some guys we were dancing with at the other bar," Julie says. "Cowboy wannabees."

The other girl tugs Julie's arm. "You coming?"

"Yeah. But I get the guy in the black hat this time."

"You can have him."

Julie gives me a point, with one finger out and the thumb up, like a pistol aimed at my heart. "So long, Jay," she says.

"Bye, Julie. Come see me again."

She turns and goes. There's a frayed horizontal rip in her jeans, maybe three inches long, just below her right cheek. I stare at that spot in the air until long after she's gone.

I'm still staring when her friend reappears in the doorway.

"Yeah?" I say.

"Just looking," she says.

"At what?"

"Nothing much."

"Thanks," I say.

"Just busting you," she says. Then she's gone, too.

So there's a guy in a black hat out there who got shot down at one place, followed his prey to Shorty's, and is dancing with Julie just because he doesn't know how to give up. Maybe I could learn something from that.

Maybe not.

"L.A. Woman"

Saturday. Spit's in the kitchen telling me about last night's performance at Ground Zero. She says they want her back real soon. She's drinking ginger ale.

Bobbi comes in to empty the bucket they dump the ashtrays into. She pours it into the trash and a puff of ashes comes up. She smiles at Spit and says, "We could use you guys tonight."

"Oh, I think they're good," Spit says, referring to the band.

"They're all right. But the crowd is down."

The band *is* pretty good, even though they're just covering popular stuff. To my ear they're as good as most bands, even some that make it. I don't know where you draw the line for success. I guess it's like basketball: the difference is that little spark of creativity, that inch more of talent. You can work incredibly hard and you'll probably get good, but then there's the extra dose of genius that separates the truly great ones from the rest of us.

"Take a break?" Spit asks.

"Sure." We sit at a table in the corner to watch the band. It's not as if the kitchen's busy. There's about nineteen people in the bar, and twelve of them would be here no matter what. So the group is performing for maybe half a dozen people.

There are four guys in the band. They're older, probably near forty, so they tend toward classic rock and some country. Two girls are dancing, and the bass player comes out onto the floor with his guitar and jives with them. He's a barrel-chested guy with a beard, wearing a black suit jacket over a red tank top, and he's got frizzy hair that's balding.

Spit leans over to me. "Check out the buttons," she says.

The guy has three shiny pins on his lapel: a guitar, a saxophone, and a treble clef.

"Merit badges," I say. "Bass, sax, and . . . general musicianship."

Spit giggles. The song ends and the bass player goes back up to the stage, which is really just a low wooden platform in the corner. He starts talking into the microphone about their Web site. Then they go into "L.A. Woman," which is a pretty good Doors tune.

Spit grabs my hand. "Let's dance."

I frown and push my chin out toward the bar.

"He won't mind," she says. "It's good for business."

I roll my eyes and shake my head.

"People will leave if nobody's dancing," she says.

I point to the two women on the floor.

"Come on," she says.

I get up and we start to dance. Spit is hard to keep up with, but I try to mirror her movements. Her hair whips around. She's skinny and quick.

She may be right about one thing, because another couple starts dancing, too. So there's six of us out there. I face the kitchen and try to be shielded by the others, because Shorty would get pissed if he saw me out here. If he happened to be paying attention.

They do "Brown-Eyed Girl" next and I start to relax. When that song ends, they say they're going to take a break, so we sit back down at the table.

A few minutes later General Musicianship walks by and Spit calls him over. He takes a seat.

"What's up?" he says.

"Hi. I'm Spit. This is Jay. Good set."
Musician camaraderie.

"Thanks. I'm Paul."

"Too bad it's slow tonight," she says.

"We're used to it," he says with a smile.

"This place can rock," she says. "My band plays here sometimes."

"Well, we haven't been together long. Takes a while to build a following."

He's sweating pretty good, so he wipes his forehead with his sleeve. "What's your band?"

"Elyit. Punk and rock, some original stuff. Depends on the night."

"Yeah," he says. "Whatever it takes."

"If you don't get 'em dancing by the second set, you're sunk," she says. "Some nights you gotta cover the Bee Gees."

He laughs. The drummer has come over, a large guy in a blue T-shirt and leather cap with a short brim. Paul jerks a thumb at him. "Dave," he says.

We shake hands and give him our names.

"Time to boogie," Dave says. They go back to the stage. I catch Shorty looking my way, so I give a little wave and go back to the kitchen.

I clean the counters and sweep the floor. Then I look out the back door for a few minutes until I hear a familiar voice. I go to the bar room and Spit's onstage with the band, doing a heightened, punky version of "Under the Boardwalk" that fills the bar. She does have a hell of a voice. I feel it right through my chest.

The bass guy is dancing with her and his guitar, and I count seven people on the floor. And when you hear the difference, the difference is obvious, what puts her above this band and most others. That spark of originality, even when she's covering an old song, that voice that's a couple of notches better than good. That thing that makes her unique.

The room is transformed.

Or maybe it's only me.

I go in the back and start making a list in my head of the positives and negatives of what I'm thinking I ought to do. The positives: she's funny, she's smart, she's incredibly talented, she's got beautiful hair. The negatives, at least the biggest ones: her reliance on drugs, alcohol, and cigarettes; her denial of all that; her history with men, at least one of them.

I make a third column, because I'm not sure which side some things should go on: her unique appearance, her attitude toward her body.

I add one last thing to the positive

column: she likes me. I'm tired of being alone.

I get up to find Spit. When I look out, she's dancing slow with somebody, some guy who wasn't here a few minutes ago.

I recognize that wide butt. It's the lawyer. I watch in awe until the song ends, then wave her into the kitchen.

"Be right back, babe," I hear her say.

She comes in and I shut the door. *"Babe?"*

She giggles. "He's not like I thought."

"No?"

"No. He's great."

"You said it was nothing. Why didn't you tell me?"

She shrugs. "This is the first time he's come around."

"So how do you know how great he is?"

"We've been killing a lot of afternoons together." She reaches over and brushes some hair off my forehead. "You know, we work until about two, then I go in and take dictation the rest of the day."

"I'm sure."

"Sorry, bud. You hurt?"

I shake my head, but I am.

"Oh," she says soothingly. "You are."

I swallow hard. "No. Just a little."

"You're sweet, Jay." She hugs me. I pat

her shoulder. "You okay?" she asks.

"Sure."

"Don't worry, bud. We'll find you somebody." She pulls back and touches my face. "You sure you're all right?"

"Yeah."

"Really?"

I nod.

"I gotta go," she says, and she kisses my cheek. "Don't wait up, Dad. I love ya."

I watch her go, then I look at the bar. One guy has his head down, dead or asleep. Another is just staring into his drink. There are four other regulars on the stools, smoking cigarettes, nursing beers. The band is playing "Brown Sugar," and there's a couple at the pinball machine, laughing and pounding the buttons.

The kitchen's closed. I've had enough. I go upstairs, take off my shoes, and lie down.

Things are not going well. I want to sleep.

But I can't.

Things suck.

And tomorrow morning I have to go to church.

Various Protestants

I have a tie, I have a jacket, I have decent shoes. I think I can get away with jeans, black ones anyway. The Methodist Church is over on Church Street, of course, about three blocks down from the back end of Shorty's. I walk over at quarter to 11.

I go up the wide cement steps. A man and a woman are at the doorway, shaking hands with everybody who arrives. The woman hands me a program and gives me a big, toothy grin. "Welcome," she says. "Glad you could come."

I stare at her briefly, wondering if I should know her. I don't. So I nod and walk into the church.

There's low organ music playing from somewhere up near the front. I see Alan in the center aisle with a small old lady on his arm. He's wearing a tweedy gray jacket and black pants (not jeans). He helps the lady into one of the pew seats and walks toward the back again. He sees me and comes over.

"Morning, Jay," he says.

"Hey."

"Follow me," he says, kind of sweeping his arm toward the aisle.

I walk behind him, then he stops about halfway up. He looks at me.

"What?" I say.

"You can sit here."

"Okay." I slide in a few feet. He starts back down the aisle.

"Where you going?" I say.

"I'm an usher," he whispers.

"Oh. I'll save you a seat."

He smiles. "I'll be in the back. I'll see you after."

The place starts to fill up. I find myself between a banker with silver hair and another frail old lady who keeps her coat on. I look around a lot during the service. I share a hymnal with the lady during "Holy, Holy, Holy," holding it open in front of her as she leans into my arm. She gives me a warm smile when the song is over.

I don't have any experience with the church routine, but I know some of the songs and the Lord's Prayer. When they pass the plates around I know enough to put in a dollar.

I shake hands with the minister on the

way out the door. When I reach the steps, Alan is waiting for me. He puts up a fist and opens his mouth wide in one of those silent yells. "You made it," he says.

I loosen my tie. "It was painless."

"Be at practice?"

"Why do you think I was here?"

"Fair enough. So we'll see you tonight."

"Yeah, you will." And I head back to Shorty's.

I show up at the Y early to shoot, but there's another team practicing. So I take a ball, sit on the bottom row of the bleachers, and bounce the ball between my feet.

Alan shows up at quarter to 6. The team I've been watching is pretty bad. Nobody can shoot, and most of them can't run much either. The eight of them are mostly medium height and kind of fat.

"Who are these guys?" I ask Alan.

He squints at the floor. "Lutherans and a couple of Baptists. Neither could field a full team so they lumped them together."

"Kind of heavy," I say.

He looks around, then leans over to me. "The tit team," he whispers.

We both laugh. "I guess the competition won't be much in this league," I say.

"Don't be too sure," he says. "There are some good players. Especially on the Catholic teams."

"They got more than one?"

"Yeah. Two Catholic teams, us, these guys on the floor, the First Presbyterians, and New Covenant."

"Who we got?"

"You, me, maybe Anthony. Peter Croce. Two freshmen I don't know very well." He counts to six on his fingers. "Robin Jacobsen and Beth somebody."

"Two girls?"

"Yeah. They're good."

"They look good?"

"You don't know 'em?"

"No."

"You'll see."

Okay, I recognize them. They're juniors. Robin is definitely somebody I've noticed. You can't help but notice her. Her pieces fit together well without any imbalances.

Beth is not bad either. She's a little shorter than Robin, a little less drool-inducing, but certainly cute.

When everybody's arrived, we sit in the bleachers and Alan steps out in front of us. "This is my team," he says. "It's not a democracy. I'll try to have everybody play at least a quarter of every game, but my intention is to win. Tonight is our only official practice. The games start Thursday. I've got schedules here. We'll play games on Sunday nights and Thursdays, and Reverend Porter is getting us T-shirts. Any questions?"

Beth raises her hand. "Who is that?" she says, pointing at me.

"A ringer," Alan says. "Jay's coming to our church now. He's very eager to get involved in the youth group, and I thought the basketball team would be a good way for him to get started."

Beth smirks. "I'm sure."

"He's very devout," Alan says, failing to hold back a smile.

Robin turns and gives me a long look. She isn't glaring, but she isn't exactly glowing with warmth either. We get up and take the floor. Alan tosses me the ball and I shoot a long-range jumper, which hits the side of the backboard and bounces out of bounds.

We run through a layup drill, and it's obvious after about fifteen seconds what kind of team this will be. This kid Peter handles the ball well, and he at least can shoot a layup. He looks pretty wimpy and won't get many rebounds, but he won't be a total liability.

The two girls are athletic and should be okay, especially if the other teams have girls, too. The two freshmen — Randy and Josh — are awkward and slow. And Anthony says he only showed up so we would have an even number to scrimmage. He'll only play in games if we get desperate.

With Alan playing inside and me bringing up the ball, we should be all right on offense. We can probably work some kind of zone on defense to minimize our weaker players.

I get a clearer picture when we scrimmage. I cover Alan, and I've got Anthony, Robin, and Josh on my side. Every time I pass to Anthony, he tries to drive to the hoop. He can always get inside Peter, but Alan cuts off the lane and either blocks the shot or keeps Anthony from shooting altogether. If he passes to Josh, it's as good as lost. He'll either dribble it off his foot, telegraph his pass and have it stolen, or throw up a shot that doesn't come within six feet of the rim.

"When you get the ball, just wait for me to come take it," I finally say to Josh. He nods several times.

The best option is to pass it inside to

Robin, who can shoot over Beth and makes most of her layups. And when she doesn't have a shot, she knows enough to pop it back out to me.

Alan and Peter work pretty well together, and Beth is all right, too. So the strategy here will be one of avoidance — keep the ball away from the klutzes.

It ought to be interesting, at least.

Sturbridge United Methodist

Th Dec 9 vs. St. Joseph's Bishops, 7:30

Su Dec 12 vs. New Covenant, 5:00

Th Dec 16 vs. St Joseph's Cardinals, 6:30

Su Dec 19 vs. First Presbyterian, 5:00

Su Dec 26 vs. Baptist-Lutheran, 7:00

Su Jan 2 vs. New Covenant, 7:00

Th Jan 6 vs. Bishops, 6:30

Su Jan 9 vs. Presbyterian, 6:00

Th Jan 13 vs. Baptist-Lutheran, 6:30

Su Jan 16 vs. Cardinals, 6:00

Su Jan 23 vs. New Covenant, 5:00

Th Jan 27 vs. Cardinals, 6:30

Su Jan 30 vs. Baptist-Lutheran, 7:00

Th Feb 3 vs. Bishops, 7:30

Su Feb 6 vs. Presbyterian, 6:00

All games at the Sturbridge YMCA

INTROSPECTION

Monday is exceptionally slow — there's just two guys at the bar, and they don't seem to have any interest in eating. So I sit at a table and watch Spit's band practice.

The band is three guys and Spit; a drummer and two guitarists. They're working on a new song; she keeps telling them to slow it down, that this one isn't like the others.

"Tease it a little," she's saying. "Build to a climax; don't just bang it out."

She sees me sitting here and smiles. "How's it sound, Jay?"

"Good," I answer.

"No," she says. "It sucks." She turns to the bass player, Kevin, who's got long curly hair and a big gut. "Don't come in right away," she says. "I'll give you a signal. I'll pump my fist or something. I'll wiggle my ass."

She nods to the lead guitar guy, Sam, and he hits the opening chords. She starts singing, soft and slow:

Staring out the window
Never even blinking
I may look introspective
But I was only thinking

There's more. She goes through the song a couple of times, then she says to take a break. She comes over to the table and sits down.

"How's life?" she asks.

I look at her sort of brightly. "Good."

"Yeah?"

"Yeah."

She drums on the table with her fingertips. "That was kind of funny the other night."

"What was?"

"You know," she says. "The other night. When you were sort of like, jealous."

"Was I?" I try to control an embarrassed smile, but it doesn't work.

"I don't know." She gives a half laugh. "Were you?"

I shrug and blush and laugh about the same way she did. "You know how Saturday nights are."

"Yeah, I do."

"And Friday nights. And Tuesdays. . . . Holidays. Weekdays. You know."

She slides her fist across the table and

bumps my arm. "My heart's bleeding for you, babe."

"Oh, so I'm the babe now, huh?"

"Hey, you got a pulse? You're my man."

Our eyes lock and we've both got silly grins. I shake my head slowly.

"Believe me, Jay, a friendship's so much better than a relationship," she says.

"I guess I don't know much about either."

"We'd drive each other nuts," she says.

"Probably."

"And you can find somebody a lot less neurotic than I am," she says, rising from the chair. She grabs my arm. "Now get your butt up here onstage with me. Let's hear what you can do."

I plant my feet. "I can't sing, if that's what you mean."

"Anybody can sing."

"Not in public."

"What public?"

I look around and roll my eyes. "I don't know your songs," I say.

"What *do* you know?"

"The *Gilligan's Island* theme."

"You know Dylan?"

"Some."

" 'Knockin' on Heaven's Door,' " she says. "Four words. That's the whole

121

chorus. I think you can handle that."

"Wait. That's technically six words. '*Knock, knock, knockin'* on Heaven's door.'"

"There, see, you know it already." She turns to the guys in the band. "We got a special guest, boys. Direct from Shorty's kitchen."

So I do it. There's no audience, no pressure, and all I have to do is join Spit on the chorus. My armpits start dripping immediately, and my voice cracks on the first "Knock, knock, knockin'," but I get through it all right; I survive.

Spit claps for me when we finish, and I shake my head and laugh.

"I'll get you up here some night for real," she tells me.

"No way."

"Yes way."

"We'll see," I say. Then I head for the kitchen. I feel lighter all of a sudden. I feel good.

Gatorade

The season runs for fifteen games; we'll play every team three times. There are three games every Sunday evening and two on Thursdays, so you get a bye every third Thursday or so.

We show up at 6 to watch the first game: the St. Joseph's Cardinals against First Presbyterian. Alan hands out our T-shirts; they're yellow, with STURBRIDGE UNITED METHODIST in blue block letters on the front.

St. Joseph's is in plain red T-shirts, but the Presbyterians have lime-green tank-top jerseys with PRESBYTERIAN in black script across the front. They also have a coach, somebody's father.

About fifteen people watch the game, mostly parents and little brothers and sisters, plus Father Jim from St. Joseph's. "Basketball's a Catholic sport," he says to one of the parents.

It would be hard to argue with that based on this game. They take a 10–0 lead right away, and win by about thirty. We play the other Catholic team next (St. Joseph's Bishops).

Alan puts us through a layup drill. He keeps saying things like "crisp passes" and "intensity." There are seven of us suited up; Anthony says he's only here for moral support.

We huddle up before the game and Alan details a strategy of sorts. "Jay, you cover Robinson. Wherever he goes, you go. I'll control the boards, you get open for the break. You other three — Peter, Robin, and Beth, you'll start — play a triangle zone with Peter at the point. Robinson's their only real shooter, so you three collapse inside a bit and clog the lane. Then just get out of the way when we get the ball. Get upcourt, I mean, and get open."

We put our fists together and shout, "Let's go!"

It feels strange trying to get up for a game like this. But it's basketball. It's my only option.

Alan wins the tap and I get the ball, dribbling slowly across the midcourt line. Kyle Robinson's guarding me. He's a senior, too. Tall and quick; a receiver on the football team and a hurdler in the spring.

There's more noise than I expected — the bleachers are half full. The other Catholic team is sticking around to watch, and there are quite a few parents.

I'm at the top of the key. They're in a man-to-man defense, and Alan is the only one of our guys trying to get open.

"Move!" I say, and Beth at least comes toward the ball. Surprisingly — maybe by accident — she sets a pick, and I drive past into the lane. I go up, find a hand in my face, and dish the ball off to Alan. He dribbles once and lays it in the hoop.

Nice. They come up and work the ball around the perimeter. They don't have a big man, but all five guys on the court are athletic. Peter gets burned badly, and his guy drives to the basket, but Alan slaps the ball out of bounds on the shot.

They inbound it, and a forward hits a short jumper to tie the score.

It's clear that Alan is going to dominate inside, so they've already adjusted their defense. The guy on Beth is leaving her uncovered outside, helping out on Alan instead. So I pass her the ball in the corner and cut to the hoop. Robinson darts over to her, and she tries to get the ball back to me. But he's got quick hands and snatches the ball away, then ignites a fast break that leads to another basket.

"My fault," Beth says.

"No," I say. "That'll work. Bounce passes, though. And quicker."

I get it inside to Alan for another layup, then steal the ball from Robinson and take it to the hoop myself. They miss a jump shot and Alan gets the rebound, fires it to me, and I take it up and hit a sixteen-footer. They call time-out.

"Not bad," Alan says in the huddle. "Let them keep it out on the perimeter if they want to. Make 'em shoot. And move it around on offense. When you get the ball, get it right back to Jay or work it inside to me. Let's go."

They keep it close through three quarters, mostly because Robinson keeps hitting three-pointers and we keep making dumb turnovers. I've dribbled the ball off my foot twice.

We're up three early in the fourth, when we finally get our fast break working consistently. Alan gets three straight defensive rebounds, hitting me on the perimeter each time, and I take it full court for a pair of layups and an easy dish to Alan trailing me for a third. The excitement level picks up; our defense gets tighter. We move the ball around, out-hustle them down the stretch, and win it by nine.

We give each other a bunch of high fives when it ends. It's nice to be 1–0. There's something at stake here, I guess.

Robin is hugging Alan, and I inch over to see if I'm next. She looks at me and gives a tight smile, but she goes straight for Beth.

I walk off and check the scorebook. Alan and I each finished with eighteen points. Peter, Beth, and Robin had one basket apiece. Good effort. I'm up. I played well. I made an impact.

I hurry downstairs to the locker room to dry my face on some paper towels. When I come up, the gym is empty. Everybody from my team is already gone. Back to the church, I guess. Am I supposed to follow?

I look around, grab my sweatshirt. They can't have gone far. I walk out into the dark, down the steps. People are milling about in the parking lot, talking by their cars. There are a couple of groups of kids about half a block away, walking toward Main Street.

I start to follow. I think I hear Robin and Beth laughing up ahead, joking around with the guys on the team. Robin, especially, looked great tonight, with ovals of sweat on her back and her chest. I get within forty feet of them and think about calling for them to wait, but then I get cold suddenly, sort of numb, and I turn up East Street, away from the direction they're going.

I fit in all right with that group on the basketball court, but I don't feel comfortable around them otherwise. Alan, maybe, but I don't know about the others. Attractive girls and church people are two groups I don't have much experience with. It's worse when they're one and the same.

I circle around the block and walk up past the hospital and the elementary school toward the supermarket. I go down the hill through the parking lot and start making a list in my head: oranges, carrots, a jar of olives, cookies. I only have a tiny refrigerator with no freezer, so I can't keep much around.

There's one of those twenty-five-cent fire engine rides for kids going back and forth outside the store, only nobody's riding it. It's moving kind of jerky and going *whump . . . whump . . . whump.*

I go through the automatic door and between two checkouts and drift over toward the fruit. This is an old store — the aisles are narrow and everything's tinged with gray. They'll be closing in a few minutes; an older guy is mopping the floor behind the deli counter.

I hesitate by the magazines and scan for anything interesting. And I spend a couple of minutes over in the fruit and vegetable area, sort of blending in with the produce. But then I just get the stuff I need and a bottle of Gatorade in the original urine color.

When I come out, there's only one light on in the parking lot and the fire engine is still going *whump . . . whump . . . whump.*

So I head for home.

SORT OF PULSATING

Monday I get another letter from my father. It's a fat envelope, but my father isn't the type to write a lot. He's included a menu, just a photocopy, from the place he hangs out in near the beach: a steak-and-pasta restaurant. They have a different dollar-beer special in the bar every night of the week. He's hand-written a note across the top: "Just like Shorty's, only a hundred times better!"

There's also an article he tore out of the *Los Angeles Times* about pickup basketball in Venice.

I take the letter to the diner. I hesitate in the doorway. Brenda — that newer waitress — is working the side to the left, so I take a booth down there. She comes right over.

"Hey," she says, recognizing me.

"Hey."

"What's up?"

"Nothing. Need dinner."

"You wanna see the specials?" she asks.

"Sure."

"I'll get you a menu."

She brings it and a glass of water. "I'll give you a minute," she says.

I decide on roast chicken with gravy.

I unfold the letter. My dad says he's getting in shape by walking and running a few miles every day, and he joined a gym. He says he thought he was in pretty good shape, "but out here EVERYBODY'S in great shape. You should see the chicks."

Yeah, I should. But I've heard all this from him before. There's a lot of stuff my father never got out of his system.

I catch Brenda's eye when she brings the food. "Your boyfriend make that?"

She rolls her eyes, glances around. "That asshole."

I give kind of a consoling smile. "Something wrong?"

"Jerk packed up and ran back to his girlfriend in Philly. The dumb shit."

"Sorry," I say. "You're staying?"

"I'm not going back there."

"No. So when did this happen?"

"Last weekend. The bitch called him up. I got pissed. He said 'screw you' and he left."

"Just like that?"

She shrugs. "We'd been fighting a lot. This is like the third time we broke up.

And the last, believe me."

I start poking at the chicken with my fork.

"I'd better let you eat," she says.

"It's okay."

"No." She looks around again. "I gotta work."

So I eat. I read the Venice article. The author is trying to be hip, trying to give an insider's take on the street ball scene out there. Trying to act like he's humbled by the athleticism on the court, but letting you know he thinks of himself as a pretty bad dude, too. What bullshit.

Brenda brings me my bill. "So you still working across the street?" she asks.

"Yeah. You gonna come by?"

"I'm underage."

"Oh."

"They check?"

"Usually." I think for a second. "Come around back sometime. I'm in the kitchen all night on weekends."

"I don't want to get you in trouble."

"It's cool. You just visit with me. No big deal. There's a good band playing this weekend; one of my friends is the singer."

She smiles. "I'll think about it."

"Okay," I say, smiling back. "Don't think too hard."

But Friday passes and nothing happens. I play ball in the afternoon on Saturday with Alan and some other guys at the Y. Then I go to work.

It's busy as hell. People are home from college for winter break and there's an NFL game on TV, so every bar stool and a couple of tables are full by the time I get in at 4 o'clock. I churn out a lot of cheeseburgers and mozzarella sticks. Time flies past. Before I know it, it's 7:30.

Spit pokes her head in. They won't go on until at least 9, but she likes to set up early.

"What's up, Jay?"

"Nothing. You?"

"Big news."

"What?"

"Got busted."

"No."

"Yeah."

"What happened?"

She starts drumming on the sandwich table. "Stanley was letting me drive his car last night after the gig. I ran a light and got pulled over. I wasn't drunk, but we had a six-pack on the floor and I tried to hide an open bottle under the seat."

"You get DUI?"

"No, I was way under the limit. Careless driving and some shit about the bottle. Stanley says I'll just get fined. No big deal."

"No?"

"Nah. I expected the cop to be a dick about it, but he was okay. Just wrote me up and told Stanley to drive me home."

I nod. "I guess there's some advantage to having a lawyer for a boyfriend."

She laughs and slaps my arm. "Oh, come on," she says. "He's not my boyfriend."

The band is great tonight. She's working in some early Beatles and a couple of Supremes songs, done unlike they've ever been done before.

I'm leaning against the kitchen doorway, just kind of pumping my hips to "Please, Please Me," when there's a rap at the back door. It's Brenda.

"Hi," she says, kind of nervous-like.

"Hi. You look great." She's got her hair down.

"I'm scared," she says, but she's smiling.

"Like I said, just stay back here."

"Yeah, but I got I.D. One of the other waitresses let me borrow her driver's license."

"Cool. She look like you?"

"Some."

She takes her jacket off and sets it on the counter. "I've never done this."

"You don't have to."

"But I want a beer."

I shrug. "Listen, you got nothing to lose. Just go to Bobbi, the woman. She might cut you a break."

Brenda starts laughing, then scrunches up her nose. "Could you do it for me?"

"Forget it. They know I'm not legal."

"Okay. I'll try."

"Good girl."

"Just give me a second." She takes a deep breath. "What was your name?"

"Jay. But don't mention me."

"Oh, no. I didn't mean that." She grips my arm. "Okay, Jay."

"Brenda."

"What?"

"Act natural."

She comes back about three minutes later with a bottle of Michelob. The place is packed, so we're shielded from the bar. We lean against the wall near the band, just a few feet from the kitchen.

The band is loud. I mouth, "wait here," and go back in the kitchen. I take off the white cook's shirt and put on my denim shirt. I get a bottle of Coke from the refrigerator and go back out to Brenda.

She points to Spit. "That your friend?"

"What?"

"Your friend!"

"My what?"

Now she screams it at me, her mouth actually grazing my ear, and I hear it clearly. I get a heated chill.

"Yeah," I say, nodding vigorously.

"Terrific voice."

"Yeah. She's . . . got a great voice." Spit's doing Springsteen's "Brilliant Disguise," fast and sort of pulsating. Brenda takes my hand and we start dancing.

When the song ends, I pull her into the kitchen. "You get proofed?" I ask.

"Yeah." She looks around and giggles. "I hand her the license, and just as she starts to look at it, the other bartender taps her on the shoulder to tell her something."

"That was Shorty."

"Yeah. So she sets it on the bar, and I discreetly pick it up and put it in my pocket. When she turns back to me, she's ready to take my order."

"Great."

"Yeah." She raises the bottle up and finishes it. "I better get another one before she forgets who I am."

"Good idea."

"Get you one

I shake my head. "I'm working."

"Oh, yeah. I forgot." She flicks up her eyebrows and walks away.

By midnight she's had four bottles of beer and we're both sweating from a lot of dancing. I've been going back and forth to the kitchen when Bobbi brings over orders, but nobody's eating much this late. Brenda's leaning into me, and we're dancing sort of fast but very close. She's singing to me, softly, and even that close I can barely hear her because of the music, but I can definitely feel her breath on my neck, her lips brushing gently against my ear. It's like a fever right down the middle of my body.

I figure I just happen to be in the right place at the right time, but I'll take it. I've been in the wrong place more than enough to balance it out.

Brenda hits the bathroom, and I go to the bar to ask Shorty if it's all right to shut down the kitchen. He says fine.

"I'll clean up everything in the morning," I say.

"You splittin'?"

"Mind if I stay?"

He looks up the length of the bar toward the front door, then sweeps his eyes over the floor. "What's up?"

"I kind of got a date."

"Here?"

"Yeah. She doesn't know how old I am."

He squints a little and studies my face. As long as he doesn't get busted he couldn't care less. "Just lay low," he says.

"Cool. I will."

"If I see you with a drink, you're gone, buddy."

"I won't. I don't."

He nods slowly. "You bangin' that singer?"

"Who? Spit?"

"Yeah."

"No way. No."

"Whatever. Have the place cleaned by noon."

"It'll be spotless."

Laundry

The sunlight hits my window, and I open my eyes after four hours' sleep. Brenda is scrunched against the wall, facedown, in one of my T-shirts and her blue cotton panties. I'm in just my underwear and it's hot as hell in here.

I get up quietly and adjust the thermostat, which is turned up to eighty. I pick up the empty condom packages (two) that I got from the machine in the men's room last night. Brenda opens one eye, then the other, and yawns.

"Hey," she says.

"Hey."

"How you doin'?"

"Good." I kneel on the mattress and she pokes my thigh. "Some night," she says.

"I'd say."

She swings her legs around and sits next to me. She grins. "Do I know you?"

I laugh. "Pretty well by now."

She squeezes my arm. "Thanks for getting me in there last night," she says.

"That was fun."

"Yeah, it was."

"I mean . . . all of it."

"Yeah. You sleep okay?"

She shrugs. "Some."

"Me too."

She stands up slowly. "Can I use your toothbrush?" she asks.

"I think that'd be all right."

She looks at me over her shoulder on her way to the bathroom. Then she stops, turns to me, grins, rolls her eyes, and shakes her head.

I spend an hour cleaning the bar, then gather my clothing in a pillowcase and walk three blocks to the laundromat. I'm down to my last pair of socks.

The third washer I look in doesn't seem to have much hair in it, so I wipe it out and dump in some detergent. I always wash whatever's dirty together — white stuff and everything else. Who cares if my underwear turns gray?

Sturbridge water is notoriously foul. No one drinks it — bottled-water companies must love this town — and on really bad days the wash comes out only semi-clean. Today it seems all right.

I could sit here and wait for the washer

to finish, but I didn't bring anything to read. There's a row of chairs along the wall across from the dryers. A fat guy about fifty is smoking a cigarette and reading the newspaper; a bleached-blond woman in her twenties, also smoking, has a young girl on her lap and is reading *Make Way for Ducklings* to her; and a guy a couple of years older than me, with fuzzy red hair sticking out from under a Bulls cap, is just staring out at the street.

I'll walk up to the deli for a sandwich. And I need to get quarters for the dryer.

We blow out the Presbyterians in the 6 o'clock game, then walk to the church for a meeting. I don't say much on the way over. In fact, this is all I say:

— "Whoa. Watch it." (When Beth stumbles slightly, stepping off a curb.)

— "Yeah, (laugh) I suck." (When Alan busts my chops about throwing away three consecutive passes in the second quarter.)

— "Maybe. . . . Probably." (When Josh asks me if I think he should try out for the high school team next year. He'd have no chance.)

The meeting is not a big deal. People play pool or Ping-Pong for a while, and others sit around and talk. I opt for pool.

Then Alan runs a short meeting about paying dues, church attendance, the need for kids to help out with set construction for the elementary-grade Christmas pageant, and some deal about caroling at the senior citizens' center. He also gives an update on the basketball team.

"The Saturday after New Year's is our spaghetti dinner to raise money for the spring retreat," he says. "I think everybody signed up for at least one chore."

He looks at me. "Jay," he says.

"Yeah?"

"You're not on the list. Can you be here?"

"I would," I say, and I mean it. "But I work every Saturday night. I have to."

"Oh. Well, you could help set up tables and chairs in the afternoon. You up for that?"

"Sure." Sounds painless to me.

"About three o'clock."

The youth minister says a few things about the infiltration of drugs into the community, even among kids a lot younger than we are. He asks Alan and one of the girls if they'd be willing to speak at a meeting of the local clergy association — he calls it the Ministerium — about drug use among high school kids. They agree to do it. Then we say a prayer and adjourn.

I play another game of eight ball with Peter and the two freshmen from the team. Alan, Robin, and Beth are among a group talking at a table with the minister guy. Eventually, they get up and start putting on their coats. Alan waves me over.

"Want to hang out awhile?" he says.

"Sure." The group standing near the door to leave is juniors and seniors: Anthony, Beth, Robin, two other girls.

We cross over to the park in front of the courthouse. There's one of those big wooden climb-on playground things for children, made from beams and steel and old tires. We sit in a tight bunch. The air is cold but still, and you can see your breath.

"So, Alan," says Tracy, who I think is vice president of the youth group. "You got any research material?"

"What, you mean that infiltration stuff?" He smirks and reaches into the inside pocket of his jacket. He pulls out two joints. He lights one and hands it to Tracy, then lights the other and gives it to Anthony.

I put up my hand when the first one reaches me. "I can't," I say. "Asthma."

Alan gives me a look. "Get out."

"Well, okay. Not asthma. But smoke kills

my throat. So I'll pass."

I've managed to avoid smoking, drinking, and otherwise ingesting every substance Spit has offered me without feeling embarrassed. Ironic that I should get put in this spot by the church group. Nobody seems to care, though. They just reach past me as they pass around the joints.

The conversation centers around parents and music and who's in trouble in school. The subject of basketball does not come up.

I say about as much as I did before, but I don't feel all that uncomfortable. Brenda told me this morning after she brushed her teeth that she'd decided to go back to her parents in Doylestown. There's nothing for her here. She said she came by last night out of curiosity — she'd never drank in a bar before. Plus she figured she had nothing to lose with me.

I guess I could feel used. I don't. I feel grateful. It felt great — not just physically — to be with someone like that. Kind of like a big meal with gravy and mashed potatoes when you haven't eaten all day.

Beth nudges me and holds a joint toward me. I put my hand between my face and her hand and smile. She sticks her tongue out at me, then leans over to Anthony and gives the joint to him. "Wuss," she whispers as she turns back to me, but she's all smiles.

"Junkie," I whisper back.

She punches my arm. I nudge her with my elbow. "There's a first time for everything," she says.

"Yeah," I say. "I know."

Noel

I guess I need to get used to being alone on the big days. Christmas Eve I stay up late, sitting by my window watching cars go by. I try to ignore the passing of midnight, but suddenly I have to face the fact that it's Christmas Day and there's no one here to wish me a merry one.

It's cold and it's raining, and the cars going by have their wipers on. There are lots of colored lights downtown, and Santas and reindeer decorations. I didn't get a tree for my room or anything.

I wish I was tired, but I'm not. I lie on my mattress and look at the ceiling.

It's stopped raining by the time I wake up. We play tomorrow night, but that's a long way off. The Y is closed, the supermarket is closed. Everybody's with their families; even Spit's staying home with her mom today.

So I've got about thirty-six hours to kill before the game. I decide to go for a walk.

It's 8:30 in the morning. I walk along Church Street, with its rutted sidewalk and big puddles. And it dawns on me that I don't have to be alone the entire day.

I cross the street and check the message board outside the Methodist Church. "Christmas Service, 10 A.M.: A Child Is Born." Good deal.

I head up to Main Street on a hunch that the Turkey Hill store will be open. It is. I get a carton of orange juice and some Twinkies and sit on a bench to have breakfast. It's good to be out. I'm hoping Beth will show up at church. Or Alan or Robin or anybody.

I go back and change clothes and kill another hour. Then I walk up to the church. There are more people than last time. In fact, it's full. I squeeze into a pew near the back and catch Alan's eye. He waves.

There's a lot more music this time, mostly Christmas music, of course, like "O Holy Night" and "The First Noel." I spend a lot of the time scanning the backs of people's heads, looking for anyone I know. I see Beth and Robin up near the front with their families.

I've heard this story before, how Christ was born in a manger and came here as the son of God to set us straight and redeem us. And it's a nice story, but I've always wondered how anyone could buy it so wholeheartedly, to accept without question that there's this being up there who loves us and forgives us, and waits for us to join him in Heaven.

There's an old couple on my right, the woman in a flowery blue dress — she seems to be just about blind — and the guy in a brown corduroy jacket over gray flannel pants. And you know they believe with all their hearts.

Next to me is a quiet guy about thirty, who keeps his eyes closed most of the service, like he's concentrating on every word, nodding slowly with his lips pursed tight.

And the minister says something about following Jesus' light by lighting the way for others. And I swallow hard and look around. The lady next to me gives me a warm smile and I smile back. We all stand for another song — "Oh Come, All Ye Faithful" — and I get a bit of a surge, like stepping to the free-throw line or something.

I don't quite believe the story. I don't see the connection from God to Jesus to me and back again. But I'm glad these people do. "Joyful and triumphant" fits the mood in here today, and it fills me, too. I'm glad I came here. And a part of me wishes I could believe. Part of me thinks I might come back sometime.

I hang around outside the church for a while after the service, talking to Alan and some others. When they start to disperse, I walk back to Shorty's.

I'm feeling all right, so I'll get this over with. I go into the bar — Christmas is the only day of the year that Shorty doesn't open for at least a few hours — and sit at the pay phone. I take a deep breath and punch in the numbers.

"Mom."

"Jay," she says brightly.

"Merry Christmas."

"Oh, Merry Christmas to you, sweet-heart."

"Having a good day?" I ask, not really wanting to know.

"Yes. Wonderful. How about you? You're not alone, are you?"

"Some," I answer. "But not entirely. I hung out with some friends for a while. Went to church."

"Church?"

"Yeah. I go once in a while. Some of my friends do. You know." I've let her think over the years that I have a bunch of friends, that I'm relatively popular. Why should she be concerned that I'm a loner? She's barely been part of my life.

"Well, I sure miss you, honey." She always says shit like that. But we avoid each other like the flu.

"Thanks," I say. "I know."

"You've got to come see us soon."

"Yeah. I will." "Us" means her and Norm, the guy she lives with in New Jersey. I've met him twice. He plays a lot of golf. Cares a lot about his car. Smokes cigars. Wheezes.

"Did you get my card?" she asks.

"Yeah. Thanks." A Christmas card with a puppy wearing a Santa Claus hat on the front, and a check for twenty-five dollars.

"Oh," she says. "Well, I miss you."

"I know."

"I'm sorry you're alone," she says.

"It's all right."

"No. It isn't," she says.

I wince a little, because her tone is starting to change. That's inevitable, but I'd hoped we could feign togetherness for a few minutes longer.

I hear her sigh. "You shouldn't be alone."

"It's not a big deal, Mom."

"I don't just mean today," she says.

"Mom . . ."

"No. Why the hell did he have to leave you like that?" she says. "He had no right."

"It's okay," I say softly. "I'm fine."

"I guess he used up all the whores in the county," she says. "Had to start looking elsewhere."

Jesus, this is all I need. "I'm not sure you're being fair," I say.

"Oh, don't go sticking up for him again," she says. "He abandoned you, Jay. He's scum."

I let out my breath, which I guess I've been holding. "He didn't abandon me. He just got on with his life. It's not like I'm nine years old again."

Everything ices up with that comment. I try an abrupt change of subject, which at least will end the conversation in a hurry. "So," I say. "Did he get you some nice presents?"

"Did who get me nice presents?"

Huh? "Norm."

"Yes. Thank you."

"Oh," I say. "Like what?"

"Gifts."

"I see." We don't say anything for a few seconds, which seems like an hour. "Well,"

I say. "You probably have a lot to do."

"I do."

"Okay, then. Merry Christmas."

"Thank you."

"And to Norm."

"Mmm-hmm."

"Okay, then."

"Bye."

I stare at the phone. And to all a good night.

When Spit shows up, I'm in my underwear, eating sardines out of a can.

"My mother said I should come check on you," she says, leaning against the doorframe.

"Really?"

"Yeah." She's got her hair pulled back in a ponytail, a look I've never seen on her. "She said to drag you out of this hole and haul you over to our house."

"What made her say that?" I set the sardines on the radiator, and look around for my pants. I'm uneasy about this. A big part of me would rather be by myself than to have anyone feeling sorry for me.

"We were just sitting around and I said, 'Shit. Jay must be all alone.' So she sent me over here."

"That's nice of her. She doesn't even know me."

"She's a great mom. She asks about you." She gives me a sweet smile. "Ever since you rescued me."

"I should bring her something."

"Forget it. We did the big gift thing last night. Today we mostly eat."

"Okay." I don't have anything to bring anyway. Pop-Tarts, maybe. Or potato chips.

It's late afternoon and the streets are empty. We walk up Main Street and turn toward the hospital. They rent the first floor of a house back here.

Her mother greets me at the door in a green dress and bare feet. They have a tree; it's small but real, decorated with a string of tiny blue lights and wooden figurines.

"Jay," her mom says. "We were ready to eat, and Sarita mentioned that you were likely to be alone."

"It's all right," I say. "I called my mother. . . . Thanks for inviting me."

"Thank you for coming."

There's braided bread on the table, which is set for four. "Can I help with anything?" I ask.

"Would you like to pour some cider

153

for us?" she asks.

"Sure. Three of us?"

"Yeah," Spit says. "That fourth one is for the ancestors. They all crowd in there together."

"I see."

Her mom gives her a playful slap on the wrist. "It's a tradition to set a place for our ancestors at Christmas dinner, Jay."

"Sounds nice."

So I go into the kitchen, which is painted in warm colors and has big ladles and tongs and things hanging from the wall, and garlic and other spices. Great kitchen. Not like Shorty's.

We eat a salad with mangoes and spinach, and then stewed fruit. Spit goes out to the kitchen and brings back a platter of fish. "It's haddock," she says. "Have to spill some blood on a holiday, you know."

"Sarita."

"Sorry, Mommy," Spit says, and she takes a little piece anyway.

A small black-and-white cat comes into the room and stops at Spit's chair, mewing up at her. "Hi, Katie," Spit says. "You can have some." She reaches down and gives the cat a fragment of the fish. The cat eats it and then plops down under the table.

"Your mother," Spit's mother asks me

after a while, "is she . . . well?"

"Yeah. . . . No. Physically, I guess. She's hard to explain. I guess I don't even know her." I look down at my plate, blink a couple of times. I don't know her, so I don't miss her. But sometimes, like here, I catch a glimpse of what I might be missing.

"Maybe when you're older you'll find a way to . . . reconnect. Sarita told me a little." She smiles at me like the older waitress at the diner, the breakfast lady. "Sarita's father is ill . . . in that same way, I think." She's rubbing Spit's arm kind of tenderly. Spit looks, what, sweet? Young. Comfortable.

And I suddenly feel very grateful to be here. Nobody's rubbed my arm like that for a long, long time, if ever, but somebody will.

I say, "I think, when my father was here looking out for me, she could pretend that I was okay. So we could at least talk sometimes. Now she knows I'm on my own, so she gets pissed at my father all over again. Like it's all his fault."

Spit reaches over and rubs my hand. The food is good. We stop talking about distant parents, and Spit's mother tells me about her early childhood in Portugal, the way her own parents loved their five children,

155

how her father worked in a cannery. I stay until late in the evening. We play cards. They teach me a carol about a farmer who is awakened by a bird and told to make preparations for the arrival of three guests.

I mean, I have guilt, too, about not being able to talk to my mother, but part of that is loyalty to my father. As big a screwup as he's been, at least he tried. He tried for a good long time.

He's still trying, I guess. I know he is.

It's snowing lightly when I leave, but there's no wind. A good night for sleeping after all.

THREE

WEASEL

I go with Alan to the Sturbridge Holiday Tournament on Tuesday evening. Sturbridge has won this thing like ten years in a row, but it's kind of shameful the way they stack the field. Tonight we're playing West Sullivan, New York, for example, which couldn't beat our freshman team. I mean no disrespect, because this is a school with like twenty-five kids in their graduating class every year. We've got ten times that many.

The "championship" game tomorrow night will be against either Forest City or Montrose, which are both small and not exactly powerhouses. While other teams look for tough early season opponents to prime the pump, our school just looks for easy wins.

Brian Kaipo scores eight points in the first quarter, and the lead quickly reaches double digits. Early in the second, he makes a nice steal and races upcourt, two strides ahead of everybody else. He can't quite dunk, but he makes a spectacular reverse layup that gets the crowd on its feet. I notice Coach stand up, too, but he doesn't look pleased. He stands there with his arms folded, glaring at Brian.

Brian steals another pass and goes the length of the court again. He could easily make another layup, but he swings a behind-the-back pass toward Jared Hall. Jared's not expecting it. The ball glances off his fingers and winds up in the third row of the bleachers.

Ricky gets up from the bench, takes off his warm-up top, and goes over to the scorer's table. He goes in for Brian, who gets a huge cheer from the crowd. Coach makes him sit next to him, and you can see him chewing him out, although he doesn't raise his voice enough that you can hear it.

Brian's arguing back. Eventually, he gets up and goes to the other end of the bench, shaking his head. He doesn't play at all the rest of the night.

After the game, Alan and I walk down Main Street to hang out by Turkey Hill, which is something I wouldn't normally do, and never would do alone. You have to have a certain credential to hang out here, a certain level of rebellion or machismo.

There's not a whole lot of things that are

less cool than being president of a Methodist youth group, but Alan seems to thrive on it. Which in a way makes him extra cool, because he's accepted in most circles in spite of that.

He starts talking to a guy named Gary who's wearing a long Army-type coat. The guy glances at me and nods.

"Weasel been around?" Alan asks.

"I seen him before," Gary says. He looks back at me, not sure if I can be trusted. "Down in front of O'Hara's."

"He got stuff?"

"He's always got stuff."

"Maybe I'll walk down that way."

Weasel is a drug dealer; Spit buys from him sometimes. He's about a year older than I am, but he dropped out of school a while back.

Gary walks away.

"More research, huh?" I say.

Alan gives a short laugh. "I just want to get a couple of joints. I'm not big into it." He bumps my arm lightly. "You up for this?"

"No," I say. "I know what would happen if I ever got started with that shit. My family's got a history."

"So you've never gotten high?"

"Depends how you look at it," I say.

161

"Basketball's my high. I'm not kidding."

So we walk a few blocks toward the center of town. "I've only bought from this guy once," Alan says. "He may act a little paranoid."

Nothing is open down this way except for a couple of bars and the Chinese take-out place, so nearly all the storefronts are dark. We find Weasel sitting in the doorway of a jewelry shop with his back to the glass. He stands up as we approach.

"Men," he says.

"Hey," Alan says. "How's it going?"

"No complaints," he says. "Have a seat."

We sit on the stoop. "You know Jay?" Alan asks.

"Jay," he says, sticking out his hand. The hand is cold and dry, sort of bony, even though the rest of him is puffy. "So what are you boys doing?"

"Hanging out," Alan says. "How's business?"

"What business would that be?"

"Whatever business you're up to."

"Well," Weasel says, looking around. "I ain't ready to retire."

"Hey, you're young."

Alan asks him how his sister's doing, and Weasel just says she's all right. A guy — an adult — comes walking briskly by, carrying an unopened umbrella. All three of us watch until he's about a block away. Nobody says anything for a minute.

"I could use a couple of joints," Alan says.

Weasel stares out at the street. "That's easy," he says.

"Same deal as last time?"

"Yeah. Same price." He looks past Alan at me. "You?"

"No." I shake my head. "I'm with him."

"Congratulations. Well, Alan, I believe I can fill your order on the spot." He pulls open his jacket and pokes around in an inside pocket. He takes out three joints, looks them over, and sets two of them on Alan's thigh.

Alan hands him some bills, and puts the joints in his shirt pocket.

"*Now* I can retire," Weasel says.

The championship is closer than the first-round game. Montrose has a big man inside, but overall they're slower and weaker. Ricky starts and plays well. There are intermittent chants of "Kai-po, Kai-po," but Brian doesn't get off the bench. At halftime we're ahead 29–22.

"This is bullshit," Alan says during the third quarter as Montrose pulls to within a point. "What's he trying to prove?"

The Kai-po chant starts again in earnest, and it seems to stir up our team. Brian stays planted on the bench, but Ricky leads a 12–0 burst, and suddenly we're comfortably ahead.

Coach pulls all the starters except Ricky with three minutes left and a seventeen-point lead. Then he calls Brian over. Brian looks around at the bleachers, then at Coach. He shrugs and walks over to the scorer's table. There's a foul a few seconds later, and Brian goes in.

The Kai-po chant stopped a long time ago. People cheer, but the excitement has worn off. In fact, I'll bet that if the chant hadn't stopped, Brian wouldn't have got in at all. This just looks like a chance for the coach to embarrass him.

First time upcourt he nails a three. Second time, too. And the third. Then he gets a steal and dribbles the length of the court, scoring a layup and finishing with eleven points in two-and-a-half minutes.

The announcer asks that everyone stay for the presentation of the all-tournament team and the championship trophy. Most of the crowd leaves anyway, but me and Alan go over to the side of the court, where Brian is leaning against the wall with a small group around him. He's got a half smile on his face, slowly shaking his head.

Jared Hall and Billy Monahan make the all-tournament team, and Ricky gets the Most Valuable Player trophy. Brian sort of shrugs when Ricky gets the award, but he claps politely. Somebody says, "Should've been you, Brian," and he smirks like he knows damn well it should've.

COMMUNITY SERVICE

Spit comes to the back door the following evening when I'm eating. I open the door and hold the hamburger up to her face, like I'm going to force her to take a bite. Big joke.

She's got a light frosting of snow in her hair. Most of the orange has faded out. I ask her the obvious question about whether it's snowing, and she says it is, a little. Her cheeks are red. She looks nice.

"It's great out," she says. "There's no wind, so it feels really warm."

"Maybe we can go out in it later."

"Yeah," she says. "Hey, I went before the magistrate today."

"And they didn't lock you up?"

She swipes at me. "Just a fine, like Stanley said. And community service. Fifty hours."

"Yeah? So what are you going to do? Carry groceries for old ladies?"

"Right. She said I should call that Y where you play basketball. I could paint the women's locker room or something. Maybe I could do a mural."

"Sounds like a good idea."

"It might even be fun."

"So what'd she say? The judge."

Spit gives a kind of pouty face, like she's thinking. "Just that I should know better. That I need to think before taking chances with my life. That's a little extreme, wouldn't you say?"

"Maybe. But it sounds like she let you off easy."

"Probably. Then Stanley tried to tell me the exact same thing. 'Think about what she said,' he keeps saying." She rolls her eyes.

She sticks her hands in her back pockets and looks out the kitchen door toward the bar. Patsy Cline is singing from the jukebox. Spit looks back at me and flicks up her eyebrows. "Four people out there."

"It's Thursday. And it's early."

"Tomorrow night, man. We rock."

"New Year's Eve."

"We'll kick ass." She winks at me. "You bringing in another date?"

I laugh and shake my head, blushing. "I wish."

"She was sweet. Too bad you drove her away."

I smirk. "Yeah, it is."

"Poor Jay. One fleeting moment of love."

"Two. But that's life."

She runs a finger down my face. I lean toward her, like I might kiss her, but she gives me a squinty look and backs away. "Hamburger breath," she says.

"That's life, too."

She sticks to her chop-busting tone, in my face but flirty. "What do you know about life?"

"I'm learnin' fast."

"It's a hell of a ride," she says.

"Isn't it?"

She starts drumming on her stomach. "I love my life. I do. Maybe not everything about the way I'm living it, but I love that I have the chance to do it. I cherish every second."

She picks up a dish towel and starts wrapping it around her hand, just playing. I like these discussions we have, these little pools of calm where she talks about her songs or her past or whatever.

"Really," she asks, "she gone for good?"

"I'd say yes. I mean, she ain't coming back. I don't even know her last name. That was a . . . I don't know. Just a thing that happened."

"Things do."

"All the time," I say.

"You just gotta be there to catch 'em."

"I plan to."

We look at each other for a couple of seconds. I always smile when I look at her. I can't help it. She can't either. And no matter what I say, however stupid or offensive, she lets me get away with it.

"Things happen," I say, crossing my arms.

She crosses her arms, too. "Some things," she says.

"Surprising things, sometimes."

"Yeah," she says. "But certain things just don't."

"Certain things do."

"Unlikely things usually don't."

"You never know," I say.

"You never know."

She leans into me, her chest pressing into mine, and gets her face about two inches from me. Her eyebrows are soft, the color of a Labrador retriever. Her expression shifts almost to seriousness, and she steps on my right foot. She's shorter than I am, maybe by two inches.

And then she does kiss me, not romantically or with her tongue, but on the lips, just briefly.

She draws her face away and locks onto

my eyes again. "Maybe someday," she says.

And she looks vulnerable for once. Up close, she doesn't look any older than me. She puts her hand up to the corner of my mouth and sweeps her fingers slowly down to my chin, over the soft stubble. I kiss her thumb.

She steps back and recrosses her arms, then laughs. "Ooh," she says. "You almost had me there for a second."

I like fresh parsley, but the bunches they sell it in are too big for my needs, and most of it would go bad in my refrigerator. So I pick it up and shut my eyes for a second, breathing it in, then place it back in the pile.

The supermarket greenery is in neat, tilted rows, garden-like, with a mirrored area behind it, and they spray the stuff with water every now and then so it stays moist and fragrant. The brussels sprouts are tight little globes with delicate outer layers.

What I take is stuff I can just rinse and eat, like bell peppers and cucumbers, the smaller, pickling kind. Carrots I buy already bagged, the tiny ones already peeled.

I linger here longer than the average customer, probably longer than anybody. I always come here first, and sometimes I come back again after getting juice and canned stuff and cold cuts in other parts of the store. It has the feel of a jungle maybe. Or a nursery.

The bar is packed for the New Year's Eve party, and Shorty's brought in a third bartender, an older guy named Roy who's helping out in the kitchen some. Mostly he's just running the food out to the bar for me.

Spit opened with an entire set of fast, old rock songs like "Seven Days" and "Midnight Confession." We're jumping. I haven't left the stove, but the music permeates the whole building. Shorty wants me to bring out trays of wings and egg rolls just after midnight, and I can shut down the grill once that's done.

Spit comes in and puts her arms around me from behind.

"Good tunes," I say.

"Sarita's all-night dance party," she says. "I'll change the pace a little later. But tonight is pure entertainment."

I turn to face her. She's looking wiry in a man's white tank top, clearly with nothing under it, and the jeans with the ripped knees. She's put crayon-red highlights in her hair.

There's a knock on the doorframe, and the attorney is standing there in a grayish blue sweater. "Hello," he says.

"Hey," she says, in a tone about as neutral as I've ever heard from her.

"Taking a break?" he asks.

"A short one," she says. She looks at her wrist, which happens to be bare, and says, "Ooh, it's getting late. Better get out there."

She punches my shoulder and squeezes past him. He takes a half step into the kitchen and just stands there for a few minutes, watching me turn hamburgers. Then he clears his throat. "Do you sense that she's settling down at all?" he asks me. "I mean, I think she's starting to mellow."

I try not to smirk too much. "Maybe some," I say, although I don't know what he's talking about.

"I think so," he says. He raises his hand in a kind of wave or salute. "Well," he says, "have a good night."

Bo stops in a little later. I've never seen Bo dance or anything; he just sort of makes his way around the room, looking like he's confiding in the guys he stops to talk to. "Everything under control here?" he asks me, taking on a mock-managerial role.

"Just swell," I say.

He nods, taking a swig from his beer. He takes off his Harley cap, brushes his hair back, and puts the cap back on. "We've got big plans for you, son," he says.

"Thanks, boss."

He leans against the doorframe, one foot in the kitchen and one in the bar room, facing out at the dancers. "Lot of flesh out there," he says.

Spit's belting out "You Can't Hurry Love," and Bo's got one leg going in time. Suddenly he straightens up and pulls his legs in tighter.

Julie steps past him into the kitchen. I haven't seen her in a few weeks. She's wearing a sweatery vest with no sleeves over a blue T-shirt, and she's got on little gold hoop earrings. I probably show a bit too much enthusiasm on my face when I see her, but I can't help it.

"Howdy," I say. Then I wince a little, which I usually do when I use words like that.

"Oh, it's only you," she says, teasing already.

"And it's only you."

"How's life?"

"Great," I say. "Where you been?"

"Ah, you know. School, the holidays. Busy."

"Playing tennis?"

"Some," she says. "You?"

"I got in a basketball league. At the Y."

"Fun."

"Yeah." I've got egg rolls in the deep fryer, so I give the basket a shake. "So, you on a break between semesters?"

"Yeah."

"You going to Florida or anything?"

"I wish," she says. "No. I'm waitressing every night till school starts again."

"How'd you get tonight off?"

"My uncle died."

"Oh. Sorry to hear that."

"That's okay," she says. "It was like seven years ago."

I laugh. "I should have tried that."

"Hey, you could still get a phone call. It's not too late."

"Nah. This is the place to be anyway. And I'll be finished in here by one."

Her eyes get a little wider. "You gonna stick around?"

"Sure. I'll be greasy and sweaty and I'll smell like cheese steaks, but so will everybody else by then."

"Or they'll be too drunk to notice."

"That too." Actually I'm already calculating. I can get the kitchen reasonably tidy in about half an hour, then race upstairs, scrub my face and armpits, gargle furiously for a minute, and put on a clean shirt and a baseball hat. But that's two hours away yet. She could easily get snagged by someone else.

"When *do* you get a night off from this place?" she asks.

"Just weeknights," I say. "Why?"

She rolls her eyes. "Duh," she says.

"What?"

"Nothing."

I start grinding my teeth. "I'm only seventeen, you know." I don't know why I say that, but I do.

"So I heard," she says. She looks around. "So am I."

"Get out."

"No, I am." She giggles. "I got a great I.D."

"You lied."

She flicks up her eyebrows and gives me a coy smile. "You work here. I didn't know if I could trust you."

"I wouldn't have said anything."

"I didn't know that."

"You aren't really in college then?"

"No, I am. But not at the U. At Weston Community."

I narrow my eyes. "And you really play tennis?"

"Yeah. I'm on the team."

"And your name really is Julie?"

"Yes."

I look down at her chest and point. "And are those things real?"

She sticks out her tongue, just the tip. "Jerk."

"Let me see your I.D."

She takes out a driver's license with a birthdate that would make her twenty-one. "It's a stretch, but it works in here," she says. "And we get into Dinger's over in Weston. No place else yet."

"You've tried?"

"Oh yeah."

"Cool." I turn in a hurry and lift the basket out of the fryer. "Shit," I say, because the egg rolls are overdone.

"Nice going," she says.

"You distracted me."

"Sorry."

"They'll be all right. Everybody's drunk, remember?"

She tilts her head. "Not everybody," she says. "Not yet." She gives me that pistol-point thing with her hand again and turns to leave. "See you later, Jay."

"Yeah, you will."

I watch her go. Then I step outside, into the alley, where it's cold and windy, and there are wispy clouds blowing past the moon. "Yes!" I say in a shouted whisper, raising my fists to the sky.

Spit comes in after the third set, dripping with sweat. She goes over to the sink and gets a glass of water, something I've never seen her do before. She drinks the whole thing in one gulp.

"Do me a favor?" she asks.

"Sure."

"Can I borrow a shirt?"

"Yeah. Come on."

We go up to my room and she pulls her shirt over her head. I avert my eyes, but then I figure she could have gone in the bathroom if she cared, so I look back.

She folds her arms but doesn't cover her chest. Round, flat tits, like an inch-thick slice of grapefruit. Dark nipples. "The shirt?" she says.

I open my closet door and point to the pile of T-shirts on the shelf. "Take your pick," I say.

She thumbs through them and picks up

the yellow basketball shirt, with STUR-BRIDGE UNITED METHODIST on the front. She tilts back her head and laughs. "This'll do."

She puts it on and heads for the door.

"Wait," I say.

"What?"

"What's with you and the lawyer?"

"Not much."

"No?"

" 'Fraid not." She shrugs. "Stanley seems to have lost sight of what brought us together in the first place."

"Which is?"

"Sex and drugs."

"Oh, yeah."

"That's all I was looking for," she says. She pulls the collar of the T-shirt up to her nose. "You ever wash this thing?" she asks.

"Yeah."

"You might use a little more soap. Come on. I've got two more sets to do."

I follow her downstairs and stand in the doorway awhile, wondering how this is going to end up. Julie is leaning against the bar, with her friend on the stool on one side of her, and a burly guy about thirty on the other. They're doing shots of some-thing. I look at the stage and I see Spit, who's been looking at me looking at Julie.

It's close to 12, so I go in the kitchen to reheat the wings and the egg rolls. I just throw them in the microwave, then put them on platters. I get Roy to help me bring them out, and we set them on tables over by the jukebox.

I'm watching Julie the whole time we're setting up, but she doesn't seem to notice. But as I push my way back through the crowd I feel a hand on my shoulder, and it's her.

"You done?" she says.

"No. But soon."

"It's three minutes to midnight."

"I know. You drunk?"

She shakes her head. "Nah, I just had a couple of beers. And one shot of Jack Daniel's."

The big TV is on over the bar, and you can see the giant lighted ball about to drop in Times Square. Julie glances up at it, then looks back at me. "I want to dance," she says.

"What's stopping you?"

"Nothing. But I want to dance with you."

"I can do that. Give me a half hour." I start moving again and she stays with me. She puts a hand up between my shoulder blades to maintain contact, and I can feel it all the way down to my ankles. We get to within eight feet of the kitchen when I find Spit blocking my path.

"Hi," I say.

She says hi to me, but she's looking straight at Julie.

"You going back on soon?" I ask.

"Right after midnight."

She's still looking kind of hard at Julie, who says hi. "You're a great performer," Julie says.

Spit hesitates, looks at me, and starts bunching up my shirt, the one I'm wearing, between her fingers. "Thanks," she says. She looks back at Julie. Then at me. She leans over and kisses me on the lips, holding it there for about four seconds. Her mouth is very warm, even feverish. "Happy New Year," she says to me. She turns to go back to the stage, but gives Julie a gentle poke in the sternum. "You too," she says.

Suddenly people start counting down from ten as midnight is about to hit. When everybody yells, Julie grabs my arms and kisses me, and I taste the bourbon. She gives me a flirty kind of smile and pushes me toward the kitchen. "Go clean up," she says. "I'm not going anywhere."

I spend about twenty minutes making

180

the kitchen look presentable, but it'll need at least another hour in the morning. I run up the stairs to my room and decide that I can shower in two minutes, gargling the whole time. Even with the shower going I can hear the music loud and clear, and I stay in there for the length of "No Surrender."

I towel off, put on fresh clothes that will smell like smoke the second I enter the bar, and run the blow-dryer on my hair until it's partly dry.

Julie's by the bar with her friends again. I work my way over and touch the back of her neck.

She looks at my damp hair. "What'd you do, go home?"

"Yeah. I live upstairs."

"You do?"

"Yeah. I got a room here."

"You mean all the time?"

"Yeah. That's home."

"Oh."

Her friend turns to me and smirks. "You again?"

"Me again. What's your name anyway?"

"Nancy."

"That's a good name," I say. "Aren't you a little young to be out this late, Nancy?"

She looks at Julie. Julie smiles and shrugs.

"What do you know about it?" Nancy says.

"I don't know anything."

"We gonna dance?" Julie says.

"Sure. You coming, Nance?"

"I think I'd fall over if I tried to stand," Nancy says. "I been on this stool for about a hundred drinks."

"Well," I say. "Happy unconsciousness."

"Thanks. Maybe I'll stagger over later."

So I dance with Julie, mostly fast, for about half an hour, until Spit takes her final break.

I ask Julie how she happens to be in college at seventeen.

"Special program. I've always been advanced academically and way behind socially," she says. "But I'm catching up."

"Guess so."

She wipes her forehead. "Let's get some air," she says.

She starts to pull me toward the front door, but I tug harder toward the back. "We can go out through the kitchen," I say.

So we go out behind the place, in that squarish dark area between the buildings.

"Cool spot," she says, looking around. You've got sort of an h-shaped open area here and we're riding the hump of it, with Shorty's behind us, facing Main Street, and the used-car building about fifteen feet across from us facing Church. The alley goes straight from Main to Church on one side, but on the other side it only comes halfway up, from Church to where we're standing. It dead-ends into the continuation of Shorty's building, the back side of apartments, and other stores. So standing here we couldn't be seen from either street.

I lean against the building and she looks up and around, at the fire escape, the window boxes, the stars. She comes over and leans against the building, next to me.

"This is the kind of spot they used to write songs about," she says. "Like 'Up on the Roof.'"

"Or 'This Magic Moment,'" I say, leaning toward her.

She rolls her eyes and laughs at such a lame come-on, but she lets me kiss her anyway. In a second we've got our arms around each other. We make out for about five minutes, until the back door swings open. It's Spit.

"Oh," she says. "Sorry. I was just looking for some air."

"Us too," I say.

She nods slowly, studying us. "Sorry," she says again. "I gotta go back on."

She leaves. I nuzzle Julie's neck. "Wanna go in?" I ask.

"Yeah," she says.

I kiss her again. "You sure?"

"Maybe not." So we make out until the music starts. Mostly you just feel the air pulsing, but it's enough to dance to, so we start moving together. Eventually, I say, "We'll be closing soon. Let's go in."

"Sure," she says.

We dance for the rest of the set. When it ends, I'm wondering if I should ask her to come upstairs, but I'm thinking I ought to wait until next time. I'll get her phone number, set something up.

But Spit comes over and puts her arm across my shoulders. "Thanks for keeping him warm," she says to Julie.

Julie takes a step back, but looks at me hard. "What's going on?" she asks.

Spit answers before I can. "Bedtime is what's going on," she says to Julie. "Come on, I'm beat," she says to me.

Julie grabs my arm, pinching it. "You're sleeping with *her*?"

"Sometimes," I say, sort of in a daze. "But we're not —"

"We're not monogamous," Spit says,

stepping between us. "But I've got the right of first refusal."

Julie looks really pissed and confused, but she just stares at me.

"Come on, stud," Spit says. "Party's over." She gives me a little shove.

"Hey," I say as Julie walks away. "Wait." She turns and gives me the finger and a sneer. She's gone.

I turn to Spit. "What the hell are you doing?"

"Come on," she says. "You want me."

"I do, huh?"

"You know you do."

"Yeah, and you've known it, too. Why did you have to pick tonight?"

"I'm a spur-of-the-minute chick, honey."

I shake my head. "What's with you?"

"Come on. You want it, you got it. I've got more to offer than she does."

I push my way toward the front door and Spit follows. But when I get to the street, Julie's nowhere to be seen. "Shit," I say. I stare up Main Street, blinking hard. The bar is emptying out, people spilling out to their cars.

Spit comes over and takes my arm. "I'm freezing," she says, a little more under control.

"Yeah, well, it's cold out," I say sharply. I

let out a heavy sigh, more like a snort.

"Yeah, it is," she says, just as sharply. "Hey, listen, Mr. Innocence. You finally get me turned around into thinking maybe we could have something, then you start groping some little bitch you don't even know."

"I know her," I say. We stand there staring at each other for half a minute, frozen. "When did I do that?" I say.

"Do what?"

"Get you thinking."

She looks away, pulls her arms real tight around her body, frowning. "I don't know. That thing about . . . unlikely things, I guess. The way you said it. The way you looked at me."

I look at the sidewalk. "I thought *you* said that."

She puts her hand under my chin, makes me look up. "You're kind of a whore," she says.

"Gee, thanks."

"Well, you act like you're on this great crusade for the perfect love, but you take it where you can get it."

"And you don't?"

"No, I do. But I don't kid myself about it."

I shake my head. "Shorty's going to lock

186

that door in a minute, and my keys are inside," I say.

"Well, I'm freezing my ass off," she says. "I need to get under some blankets."

All right, I'll share my bed, but the magic moment passed a long time ago. I mean, I'm not planning any trips to the vending machine.

We go upstairs. She uses my toothbrush, which makes three of us now. I stay in the bathroom longer than I need to, staring at my reflection. I can't believe I blew it with Julie. And now the one who screwed it up is lying on my mattress.

I climb into bed. She leans up on her elbow and looks at me sort of sorrowfully, but then she kind of drops herself on me and puts her tongue in my mouth. And we start groping, and of course I get aroused, but it's nothing like it was downstairs a little while ago.

We do have sex, rather horribly, and I almost feel as if I'm being attacked. I can't help thinking about Julie — not imagining that I'm with her, but just distracted because I'm wondering if I could have been. I don't have any idea what Spit's thinking about, but it sure doesn't seem to be me.

When it's over, I get up and go to the

bathroom. I turn on the light and look in the mirror again, and I can't help frowning at myself. Or maybe just at the situation. I brush my teeth again and pull on some sweatpants, and go back and sit on the radiator, staring at the ceiling.

"Sorry," Spit says softly.

"It's okay. You got nothing to be sorry about."

"Don't I?"

I look at her. "What's wrong?"

"I don't know." She sits up on the mattress and leans against the wall. "I guess it was my turn to be jealous."

"How come?"

"I don't know. Something about that girl you were with."

"Like what?"

"I don't know," she says again. "Like maybe she was going to take you away."

"Why would she do that?"

"Why shouldn't she?"

"Well, I hardly know her."

"Looked like you were *getting* to know her."

"I guess I was."

She lies down on her stomach with her face in the pillow and looks up at me.

"You've seen me with girls before," I say. "Once, anyway."

"Yeah. I know. This one seemed different. I've just been feeling vulnerable the past few days. I got a late Christmas card from James."

"Him again?"

"It's not him. It just made me feel alone. I get that way sometimes."

"Everybody does."

"I know." She sits up and hugs her knees. She gives me a shy smile. "Sorry about the sex," she says.

"Why?"

"I mean I'm sorry it wasn't any good."

I huff. "I guess I share the blame."

She stands up and goes to the closet to get another shirt. "I think I'll go home," she says. "Okay?"

"Sure. I'll walk you."

"That'd be nice."

She stands there naked, clutching a T-shirt to her chest. She looks fragile for a second, or scared maybe. "Sorry I screwed things up with that girl," she says. "I'll explain it next time I see her."

I give a halfhearted laugh. "You think she'll ever come *here* again?"

She thinks about it a second. "Yeah, I do," she says. She bites on her lip, nodding slowly. "If she's got any fight in her, she will."

LOCKERS

We stay unbeaten with a win over New Covenant, the most polite team in the league. They've got purple shirts with no numbers, just a white cross in the center. They're Fundamentalists, and most of their players go to Wayne Christian Academy, a tiny school outside of town. I heard that their minister was actually the driving force behind the league. They draw more spectators than any other team — most of their congregation shows up for the games.

Anyway, they're not a bad team and they keep it close for three quarters. Alan finally wears them down inside and we pull away.

I'm surprised to see Spit when I walk off the court, sitting on the edge of the bleachers near the door.

"What's up?" I say.

"Wanted to see you play. Great performance. . . . I wanna show you something."

"Okay."

"Downstairs."

"Here?"

"Yeah, I started the mural." We head down the stairs toward the locker rooms. "I had to paint the room for real first, but they said I could do some artwork if I keep it tasteful. I've got most of it sketched out."

I have to wait in the hallway for a few minutes because there are some women in there. Beth and Robin come out and say nice game, and I say so, too.

"Trying to get a peek inside?" Beth says.

"I was," I say. "But I guess I missed you."

"Too bad," she says.

"Some other time, maybe."

They both laugh and keep walking.

An older woman in a blue sweat suit comes out of the locker room and Spit waves me in. "All clear," she says.

The paint smell is noticeable and the walls are covered in fresh pale yellow. There are rows of lockers on the two longer walls, and a horizontal mirror on the half wall that separates the changing area from the showers. The back wall is open, and you can see where Spit's roughed out some figures with a pencil.

"This is Patsy Cline," she says, pointing to a woman with a kind of cowboy jacket. "Diana Ross. Billie Holiday. Carole King. Margo Timmins."

I recognize most of the names.

"They're pioneers, you know. I still have to add a few. But they're my musical heroes. Pure guts, the way I see it."

"You putting yourself in there?"

"No way," she says with a laugh. "I'm no legend."

One of the employees sticks her head in the doorway and does a double take when she sees me. "We're closing," she says.

Spit smiles at her. "I was just showing my friend the artwork," she says.

"No problem."

It's snowing lightly when we get outside. My hair is damp from the game, so I pull up the hood of my jacket.

"Get some pizza or something?" she asks.

"Sure."

She's sort of quiet as we walk up toward Main Street. I am, too. This is the first I've seen her since the other night, when things broke the wrong way. It's kind of hanging in the air between us.

So we stare at each other over the pizza — not hard stares or blank ones, just studious.

She breaks a piece of crust off the pizza and turns it over in her fingers. Then she takes a nibble from it, keeping her eyes on me. "My father," she says, "would like this place. He's the type of guy who likes to sit and eat pizza, listening to lost-love songs. Wishing he was a better man, I think. It broke his heart when my mother finally left him. Even though he knew he deserved it."

"He did?"

"Yes. He's a good man, as good as a man who hurts his wife can be, anyway."

"So what does that mean?"

"Oh," she says, glancing at the ceiling, tightening her lips for a second, "like he knows he always hurt us, but he was desperate to keep us anyway. Like he can't allow himself to depend on anything to last."

She looks away again, toward the front of the restaurant, but her gaze slowly settles toward the floor. "It infected me, too." She looks up again, fixing her eyes on me. "I have trouble trusting. So I screw up, trying to drain everything I can from a moment or a connection . . . before it slips through my fingers and I lose it."

She starts to fight back a smile, then gives me that scrunched-up look again. "Then I overanalyze the hell out of everything." Her whole faces brightens and she laughs. "I get hung up on making everything right, every relationship. And it never

193

happens. I'm estranged from my father, I can't cut loose emotionally from James. Shit, I even feel guilty about Stanley. The guy can't figure out why I iced up all of a sudden. I don't have the heart to tell him I never cared. That he was just in the right place for a while."

She giggles again.

"Painful, huh?" I ask.

"Nah. Just dysfunctional."

"Join the club."

"Oh, I joined a long time ago, bud." She shakes her head with that half smile and her eyes get a little wider. "My body tends to get ahead of my brain."

"Me too, I guess." There's a light constellation of freckles across the bridge of her nose, almost golden in color. Her eyes are pale brown, and there's only the slightest change in color from her lips to the skin surrounding them. These are the sorts of details that never register with me. I usually take a whole picture. I couldn't tell you the eye color of a single person if I wasn't staring at their face.

I don't know much about trust either, I suppose. "Seems to me if you trust somebody, you usually get burned," I say. "I mean, I'm way the hell removed from being nine years old, but, you know, I can see how badly my mother could have screwed me up. Leaving like that. Could have screwed me up bad. 'Cause you know, when you're nine, like, you're supposed to be able to trust your parents at least."

She gives me a look, sort of a smile, but one of those looks that says I'm full of shit.

"What?" I say.

"She *could have* screwed you up, Jay?"

"Yeah, well . . . okay. But I think I've got a pretty good handle on it."

"All things considered, yeah. I guess you do. But don't go telling yourself you're uninjured, buddy. Don't go thinking you're okay."

I'm more okay than she thinks I am. I mean, I only mentioned my mother because she brought up her father. Yeah, I think about it sometimes, being the only seventeen-year-old around who's living alone. But I'm more together than either of my parents ever was. I can take care of myself pretty good.

"So how do I put you right?" Spit asks, jolting me out of my thoughts.

"Huh?"

"I feel like I need to erase the other night somehow."

I give her a little frown. "It's okay. I

don't think you can do that."

"Oh," she says, rubbing her foot against my shin, "I think I can."

I dwell on that a moment, crossing my arms and feeling my face start to flush.

She narrows her eyes, parts her lips. "I can't let that little episode just sit there and fester."

I try to look at this objectively, but it isn't easy. Things go through my head, like two wrongs don't make a right, but I'm not sure that applies in this case. I'm hoping not.

I motion with my head toward the door and we get up, leaving half the pizza. I'll sort this out later.

At least I'll try.

We're tender this time, slower and involved with each other. We undress each other as we go, stroking and mouthing and whispering. We're two screwed-up individuals, but when I sink into her I feel cushioned and understood and like I'm floating in a warm, gentle sea in the darkness.

It's enough to make me forget about Julie almost entirely.

THE NEXT BISHOP

I can tell something's up when I get to the Y on Thursday. There's already a crowd, and three of our players are standing under the basket, looking down the court.

"What's going on?" I say to Peter.

He just points. Brian Kaipo is down at the other end, shooting jumpers, in the same blue T-shirt as the other guys from the Bishops.

I raise my eyebrows. "What's the deal?" I ask.

"They say he's eligible," Danny says.

Alan enters the gym, and I wave him over.

"I know about it," he says. "It's legitimate. He quit the varsity today."

Okay. We're undefeated and these guys are 4–3, so they've got some work to do if they're going to catch us. But suddenly the whole picture has changed.

"Can they add a guy this late in the season?" I ask.

"The rules say until the eighth game,"

Alan answers. "So, yeah."

Right from the start it looks like a long night. I get burned on a give-and-go, then they steal the ball from Danny, and Kaipo hits a three-pointer. They go into a full-court press and Danny gets trapped in the corner again.

I race toward that sideline and catch an elbow in the cheek. But I get to Peter and he gets me the ball with a weak bounce pass.

I break the press by myself, sprinting upcourt. Alan sets a screen and I drive underneath, but Kaipo cuts off the lane and I'm stuck. I shoot anyway and he gets a hand on it, tipping it to Robinson. He scoots downcourt with Kaipo trailing, and then dishes it to Brian, and it's 7–0 after about forty-five seconds.

Alan calls time-out and jogs to the bench. The rest of us are stunned, and we stand on the court for five seconds before walking over.

"They can't keep that up," Alan says.

"Don't be too sure," I say. "He's on."

"Everybody just settle down," he says. "When they score, I'll inbound the ball. Jay, I'll be looking for you. If we let them play up-tempo, they'll run us out of the gym. So let's play smart and make them work. They wanna run all night."

And they do. I miss a jumper next time up and Robinson gets the rebound inside. He tosses an outlet pass to Brian, who dribbles to the key, makes one pass, gets to the corner for a return pass, and hits another three-pointer. It's 10–0 and he's got all of them. Everyone in the bleachers — maybe thirty-five people — is standing up and applauding.

Alan gives me the ball. No press this time. I dribble slowly across the midcourt line. Nobody's open. Kaipo is crouched low, hands up, eyes on my waist.

I get the ball to Robin; she's covered by a short, slow guy with glasses. She makes a nice move and gets a step on him, driving to the lane. Robinson comes out on her and she bounces it to Alan, who lays it in, and we're finally on the board.

I slap hands with Robin as we hustle back. "Sweet," I say.

Alan yells, "Defense, now!" I concentrate harder.

They get it inside to Robinson, and Alan fouls him on the shot. He makes the first free throw, but misses the second.

I get the rebound and start to run, but pull back because all of my teammates are behind me. I dribble a long time past the three-point arc, waiting for somebody to get open.

Finally I pass it to Robin again and make a quick cut inside. She gives me a nice feed, and I hit a short running jumper in the lane.

We go back and forth the rest of the half, holding their lead down to six or eight points, never getting closer but keeping it within reach. Kaipo keeps scoring, but they don't get any more big runs like that opening minute.

They start out hot in the second half. Kaipo hits three straight three-pointers and they build the lead to fourteen. Alan takes another time-out. "Let's go to a triangle-two," he says. "Kaipo and Robinson are the only ones handling the ball, and Robinson's staying inside. You three," he says, addressing Peter, Robin, and Beth, "play that triangle out front and help Jay with Kaipo. Just get in his face. I'll stay home with Robinson."

It works, some. Kaipo sees the situation and makes a few good passes to the open players, but that mostly results in missed shots. We chip away at the lead and bring it down to nine by the end of the third quarter.

"Go back to a man-to-man," Alan says between quarters. "Kaipo's gonna start shooting again, I guarantee it. Jay, the man is gonna score. But if you stop him a few times we'll get back in it."

A few times, yeah. Maybe one out of five. But we do trim the lead — Alan gets a couple of layups, I hit a three, even Danny nails a fifteen-footer. Two minutes left and we're within five points.

Kaipo's dribbling with his left hand, slowly pushing his right hand out and back. He's signaling to his teammates to clear out of the lane, wanting to go one-on-one with me.

He steps back, gives me a head fake, and drives left. I stay with him, hands up, bumping him with my body. He stops his dribble, leans toward the basket, then eases back and lofts a fall-away jumper over my outstretched hands. It swishes.

I bring it up quick. Alan's got position inside and I give him a hard bounce pass. He pivots and lays it over Robinson. The margin is back to five.

Kaipo dribbles for half a minute, staying outside, not risking a pass. There's no shot clock, of course, so he can dribble out the game if he wants.

"Pressure!" Alan yells, and I go for a

steal. He easily gets around me, but Peter comes up and gets a hand on the ball. It's loose and I scramble after it, grabbing it at midcourt. I call time-out.

"How much time?" Alan yells to the scorer's table.

"Forty-two seconds." We're still down by five.

"Okay," Alan says as we huddle up. "We don't need a three yet. We need two scores. Take the best shot, Jay, or get it to me inside. After we score, play tight defense. Peter — great play back there — double up on Brian. Let's go!"

Peter inbounds the ball to me and Kaipo is in my face. I dribble in, protecting the ball, needing to shoot in a hurry. I give a quick fake and shoot from behind the arc. I can tell it's off right away.

"Short!" I yell. Alan gets the rebound and I'm cutting down the lane. He dishes it to me and I duck under Robinson, hitting the layup despite getting whacked. There's no whistle.

They call time-out. We've cut it to three.

Brian takes the ball and dribbles outside again. He doesn't have to shoot; we have to foul. I go for his arm but he darts away, and I run into the short guy setting a pick.

I finally catch him and go for the steal,

bumping him hard. The ref blows his whistle. Brian goes to the line for a one-and-one.

"How much time?" I holler.

"Six seconds."

Shit.

Brian makes the first but misses the second. Alan gets the rebound and throws an overhand pass to me at midcourt. I get it and shoot, but it's way too late and the shot doesn't come close. So much for an undefeated season.

We sit in the bleachers after the game. "Not bad," Alan says. "One loss won't kill us. We hustled."

"I sucked," I say.

"You did all right on him."

"Bullshit," I say, shaking my head. "He must have had fifty points."

"Forty-five. But you're not gonna shut him down," Alan says. "It's a matter of degree. You hold him to forty and we win that game."

I look up at the ceiling. I sucked.

Beth speaks. "He's a great player."

"Yeah," I say. Great. But what does that say about me?

"We'll get another shot at them," Alan says. "He was on fire tonight. It won't always be like that. You know how you get in a groove sometimes."

I'm spent physically and emotionally, so I stay in the bleachers to watch the second game. Turns out I finished with twenty-three points, which is my high for the season, but I don't remember many of them.

Halfway into the first quarter, Kaipo comes up, showered and changed, and sits next to me.

"Good game," he says.

I smirk. "You pissed all over me."

"I was up. I hadn't had a chance to really play in about two weeks."

"What happened?"

"Ah, it's been coming," he says. "No big scene, really. I just told him I didn't need any more lessons, and if he wasn't going to play me, I might as well give it up."

"And he agreed?"

"He gave me some shit about accepting my role, but it was pretty clear I was finished."

"So here you are," I say.

"Here I am. It's okay. There's enough talent here. You're better than half the guards in that league."

"Thanks."

"Hell, we could put together an all-star team from this league and beat the varsity."

"You think?"

"Definitely. There's at least four of us who ought to be playing there anyway." He points at Donny Colasurdo, from the other Catholic team, who's bringing up the ball. "He could. And you and Alan should be. And I'm sorry, but that kid Ricky should not have my starting job. No way in hell."

"That's obvious."

He shakes his head. "Coach did the same thing two years ago when I came along — screwed a senior out of a job so I could take his place. What did I know?"

He looks out at the court a few seconds, scratching his chin. "See, Ralph doesn't like coaching seniors. I was his boy when I was a sophomore, too. It's easy that way. If you win with young guys, everybody loves you. And if you lose with young guys, it's okay, because you're building for the future. But his future never gets here because he's in a constant building mode. There's always some great sophomore who's gonna light it up in a few seasons. But Ralph can't coach, so that kid never develops. And when he gets to be a senior, the coach is already looking at somebody else. He knows if he plays the seniors and loses, he looks like a bad coach, which he is. So he invents attitude problems, says guys like me don't want it bad enough."

He laughs and turns his head toward me. "So screw it. I don't need that rah-rah shit. Next year I'll get on the team over at Weston Community College."

He slaps me on the back and gets up to leave. "I don't need an audience, man," he says. "I just wanna keep playing ball."

NOT TOTALLY PARANOID

Spit and I quickly fall into a pattern of finding each other at the end of the evening and spending the night in my room. It's a good week physically, but something isn't right. I'm afraid I'm becoming her latest addiction. I don't want her to become one of mine.

On Tuesday I go alone to the diner. I haven't been in here since Brenda left. It doesn't look like they've replaced her.

I didn't bring anything to read, so I just look out at Main Street while I eat. This town shuts down at dusk except for Turkey Hill and a couple of drugstores. Summer's different, with all the vacationers in the area, but nine months a year it's fairly bleak.

I ran into Dana today in the cafeteria at school. Sleep has become more of a necessity lately, so I haven't played on a Tuesday morning in weeks. I was really more interested in checking her out than playing hoops at that time of day anyway, and there've been just too many others on my mind to even think about her. Physically she'd be a great match for me, but I think her general maturity might be a problem.

I don't know why, but I decide to call my father. I haven't talked to him in a month.

He picks up on the third ring. He sounds upbeat, a little out of breath.

"Just this second got in from the gym," he says.

"You lifting weights?"

"No. Just hanging out. Treadmill. Checking out the women."

"Oh."

"You doing all right?" he asks.

"Yeah."

"Things are looking up?"

"Yeah, I guess."

"I left a couple of messages at the bar. Shorty ever tell you?"

"He usually remembers about a week later."

"That's him," he says. "Thought I'd hear from you on Christmas, though."

"Me too. Then I got busy."

"Yeah? Did you go to your mom's?"

"No. . . . No, I just called her."

"Oh."

"Yeah."

"So how'd that go?" he asks.

"Pretty much like you'd expect."

"Mmmm. I can imagine."

"The usual guilt trip."

"I been there, buddy. I been there."

We're quiet for a few seconds. Phone silences, even short ones, always leave me feeling empty.

"She bitch about me?" he asks.

"Yeah."

"That figures."

"I know."

"Listen," he says, "I had my life on hold for almost ten years, Jay. I'm forty years old. I'm losing my hair. I was tired of being alone."

"Dad, I know all that. I don't blame you."

"I know you don't. I would have stuck out the year if I didn't think you could handle it. But I'm still carrying some guilt about it."

"Yeah. Well, she ought to be carrying a whole lot more than you are," I say.

"I'm sure she is. Maybe not on the surface, but it's got to be there somewhere."

"Pretty deep inside, I'd say."

"That can be the worst place."

"True," I say. "Hey, if I thought she was capable of being a parent, I'd hold it against her for not trying."

I think he laughs a little. "Sometimes I think you're more mature than either one of us," he says.

I'm not going to argue that point. "I'm doing fine," I say. "I'm playing a lot of hoops. Staying out of trouble."

"Me too, unfortunately."

"No prospects, huh?"

"Maybe a few. More opportunities than in Sturbridge, that's for sure."

"Hey, your wife said you screwed around here plenty." I'm trying to make a joke. I can tell right away how flat it falls.

"Well," he says hesitantly. "She exaggerated that."

"Exaggerated it or made it up?"

"A little of both," he says. "She wasn't totally paranoid. Those accusations were . . . well, they had some merit, I suppose."

More silence. He clears his throat. "How about you?" he asks.

"What?"

"You seeing anybody?"

"Um, yeah, sort of."

"Glad to hear it."

"Yeah," I say. "It's not like . . . I don't know. Not a complete package."

"How so?"

"I don't know. I guess . . . I'm not in love. Not with her anyway."

"Hey. Don't let that bother you," he says. "I mean, you're not even eighteen years old yet. You'll think you're in love ten times before you even know what it is."

"Only ten?"

He laughs. "If you're lucky. Hell, if you do figure it out, be sure to let me know."

I head for the Y about an hour early on Thursday to shoot. We're playing the tit team, which we beat by twenty the first time around.

Spit's in the gym when I get there, talking to two little girls in leotards. She waves. I pick up a basketball and start dribbling.

I go down to the far end and shoot chippies, just rebounding and laying it in off the backboard. After a minute Spit comes running down.

"Pass," she yells, and I bounce the ball toward her. She grabs it and shoots it over the backboard. "Pretty close," she says.

I chase the ball down. "What are you doing here?" I ask.

"Working with those kids," she says. "I finished the mural and I still owed like five hours. They were starting gymnastics practice when I was ready to leave, so I asked if I could help out."

"That's good."

"Yeah. I'm rusty, but I got up on the beam. The girls are adorable."

I shrug. "Do me a favor," I say. "Rebound for me while I shoot free throws."

"Check."

Alan shows up about twenty minutes later, and the rest of the team follows soon after. Alan says he and I won't start, since this is an obvious mismatch and we've played nearly every second of every game so far. Baptist-Lutheran is winless.

So we sit on the bench and watch as we fall behind by a couple of baskets early. No cause for concern, but we've got no size on the court, and our opponents are moving the ball around better than usual. Alan tells Beth to call time-out about midway through the first quarter with us trailing 8–4.

"Peter," he says in the huddle, "you've got to push the ball up the floor. These guys are slow as shit, and we should get some easy transition baskets. Tighten up the defense, too."

Beth asks when me and Alan are coming in.

"Second quarter," Alan says. "You guys

get some work in first. We'll be fine."

But we're down by eight when Alan and I check in. It's been mostly amusing, although we figured the others would at least hold them even. No sweat.

I match up with their best shooter, a junior who can hit from the outside if he's open. He won't be.

First time down I chuck up a long three-point attempt, but it bounces off the rim and they get possession. "Cold," I say to Alan as we run back.

"No problem," he says. "Work it inside."

I guard my man tight while they move the ball patiently around the arc. He gets the ball and gives a kind of stutter step, then lofts it over me. It caroms off the backboard and into the hoop.

I smirk at Alan as he inbounds the ball. "Time for a little run," I say. I bring it up and dribble in place at the top of the key, between the legs and all. I can take this guy easy. I drive the lane, give a little juke, and send a soft left-hander toward the rim.

Rejected. Somehow one of their guys gets a hand on the ball and slaps it up-court. They chase it down and pull back, setting up their offense again. They've been practicing.

Their heaviest guy drives the baseline,

and Alan scoots over to cut off the lane. The guy makes a neat bounce pass to my man cutting in, and he lays it off the board for two more.

I shake my head, but I still give a little smile as Alan passes it in to me.

I get the ball inside to Alan and he scores easily. Then Danny gets a steal and hits me on the run for a layup. They call time-out. We're trailing 18–10.

They slow it down a lot, passing around the perimeter and eating up the clock. I hit a couple of threes and Alan gets some inside points, but they're still up by five at the half.

The frustration continues in the third quarter. We're flat as can be, probably because of the emotional letdown after the near-comeback against Kaipo's team. And it doesn't help that I keep throwing the ball away. I've always had a habit of tele-graphing my passes, but it's worse when my focus isn't right. Tonight I just want to get this over with, make one big run to put these guys away, then forget this game ever happened.

I get a couple of steals early in the fourth quarter and hit a driving layup and a short jumper. Then Alan gets a defensive rebound and hits Peter with a long outlet pass, and Peter gets it inside to me for another layup. That gives us our first lead of the game, 36–35.

They call time-out. Alan says not to lose the momentum now that we've finally got it. "We lose this game, we suck," he says.

But suddenly we turn ice-cold again. They change their defense to a box and one, keeping a guard on me all the time and doubling up if I drive. The man on me is deceptively quick I discover after he slips his hand in a couple of times and smacks the ball away. I recover the first time, but the second time they get control and it leads to a layup that gives them back the lead with about a minute to play.

We call time-out, down by a point. "Hold for the final shot," Alan says. "Jay, work it in to me or take an open jumper. The rest of you crash the boards. They'll be doubled up on Jay and me, and one of you might get an easy put-back. Now suck it up or be embarrassed. Let's go."

Alan inbounds to me and I dribble up slowly. They try to trap me at midcourt, but I get around it easily. I whip it to Alan, but he hasn't got good position, so he kicks it back out to me. I keep dribbling, then take another time-out when the clock gets down to twelve seconds.

"Okay," Alan says. "We want to shoot when it gets under eight. We have no time-outs left, so don't try to call one. Be smart. Twelve seconds is a lot of time."

I inbound the ball to Alan to be absolutely safe, and he gives it right back. I drive to the free-throw line, give a quick fake, then unleash a running jumper that circles the rim and falls out. There's a scramble for the rebound. For an instant Alan has it, but he loses control and the ball bounces toward the corner. Peter grabs it and fires a wild, off-balance shot that doesn't reach the rim.

The fat guys go wild.

We just stand there stunned.

Ground Zero

I don't think I've been in the guidance office since I was a freshman, but I stick my head in there between classes on Friday and ask the secretary if I can have a Weston Community College application. I figure I should at least look it over. Keep my options open.

I mentioned to Alan the idea of possibly playing ball there next year, but he's already been accepted at Yale. Kaipo's going, though. And Julie's there.

I lean against some lockers and glance at the application.

This does not look like a great weekend ahead. Spit's band is playing over at Ground Zero tonight and tomorrow, and there'll be a DJ at Shorty's again. It'll be boring as hell. I've been praying that Julie will show up, give me a chance to explain.

What is it I hope to explain, though? That I wasn't having sex with Spit. That at that moment of misunderstanding I was innocent of wrongdoing, and was free and clear to pursue any and all possibilities with Julie. Clean as a whistle, I was.

Spit and I haven't talked about this. She had promised to talk to Julie, of course, but the chance hasn't come up. And there have been numerous intervening escapades since then. So I'm not sure if Spit would try to kill me or not. Or kill Julie. But I think the sex thing is fizzling out in a hurry. At least from my point of view.

"Hey," somebody says.

I turn and it's Beth from the team. "Hi," I say.

"What'ya got?"

I show her the application.

"You going there?" she asks.

"I don't know. I don't have any idea what I'm doing next."

"I don't envy you," she says. "Well, in a way I do. You'll be out of this school in a few months. But I'm sort of glad I've got a while longer to figure out what I'm going to do."

"Well, I'm in no hurry either. I already got a job. Or I can go to California to be with my dad. Whatever. I was mostly thinking about college so I could play bas-ketball."

"Yeah, I can't imagine you without it," she says. "Oh, shit. I'm late as hell for class." She starts running off. "See you Sunday night," she says.

We play the Cardinals on Sunday. We need a win pretty badly.

I don't see Spit all weekend. Work is as expected both nights, dreary and lonely. There's never more than twenty people in the bar. Shorty lets me shut down at 11 both nights.

So Saturday at midnight I go out for a walk, just up and down Main Street once. There are a couple of small groups of kids hanging out, one group huddled in a doorway down by Seventh Street, and the other by the bench near Turkey Hill.

That night I have that dream I most fear having, the one where it's resolved in your favor, when she tells you that you're the one she wants, and for an instant you're the happiest guy in the world. Then you wake up, look around the room, and for a long, long time you're the saddest.

I don't even know who I was dreaming about.

NEW SNEAKERS

We've fallen into a tie with the Cardinals because of our two recent losses, and we play them tonight with first place on the line. We beat them last time, but it was close.

Kaipo's got his team right on our asses, too. I get to the Y early and check the bulletin board:

STURBRIDGE YMCA
CHURCH LEAGUE STANDINGS

As of January 13

	W	L
Sturbridge Methodist	7	2
St. Joseph's Cardinals	7	2
St. Joseph's Bishops	7	3
New Covenant	4	6
First Presbyterian	2	7
Baptist-Lutheran	1	8

SCORING LEADERS

	Points	Games	Avg.
Brian Kaipo (SJB)	127	3	42.3
Duane Olver (NC)	174	10	17.4
Jay McLeod (M)	155	9	17.2
Don Colasurdo (SJC)	136	9	15.1
Alan Murray (M)	131	9	14.6

LAST WEEK

Bishops 72, Cardinals 58
Methodist 51, Presbyterian 45
New Covenant 53, Baptist-Lutheran 37
Bishops 68, New Covenant 44
Baptist-Lutheran 37, Methodist 36

THIS WEEK

Sunday: 5:00 Bishops vs. Baptist-Lutheran
6:00 Methodist vs. Cardinals
7:00 Presbyterian vs. New Covenant
Thursday: 6:30 Baptist-Lutheran vs. Presbyterian
7:30 Cardinals vs. New Covenant

Kaipo toys around with the Baptists in the first game, scoring about twenty-five before halftime. I sit in the bleachers with Alan and Beth.

Alan barely says anything. You can tell he's psyching himself up, because he's staring at the court with his mouth kind of hard, shutting his eyes every few seconds. Last year when we were playing JV, he would throw up before some of the games, especially the ones that figured to be close. He said the jitters usually went away after that.

I'm feeling edgy, too, but I don't think I show it like he does. I tend to gradually focus in on the game over the course of the day. Right now I'm about ninety percent there. By game time, I'll have tuned everything out.

Beth nudges my knee with hers. "Big game," she says.

I turn my head halfway and look at her. "True," I say. "I think every game is gonna be big the rest of the way." I point out at the court. "It's gonna come down to us and them," I say, meaning Kaipo's team.

"You think?"

"Yeah. I mean, who else is gonna beat them? The way he's playing."

She nods. "He's great. And he's such a

nice guy, too. He never acts like he's a star. I love watching him play. He's so fluid."

"Yeah. Smart too. He almost never makes a mistake."

Alan finally speaks, still staring straight across the court. "You can stay with him, Jay. You might not shut him down, but you can neutralize him enough for us to beat them. You just gotta step up. But that's two weeks away yet. Let's think about tonight."

Tonight turns out to be intense. I'm guarding Donny Colasurdo, who's my height but more muscular from playing football. He and I play at about the same tempo, ready to run the fast break when the opportunity arises, but content to set up and drive and play the other guy tight.

It's close throughout — neither team can get ahead by more than three or four points. Alan nails a baseline jumper with about six seconds left to send it into overtime.

We huddle up and I wipe my face with a towel. It's been a physical game and Alan's got four fouls. The bleachers are full. The first two teams stayed around because this one's for first place, and the other two are waiting to play. Plus New Covenant's got its whole contingent of fans waiting, so there's a lot of noise coming at us. "Play tough defense," Alan says. "Fight through the screens."

Alan taps it to me off the jump ball and I shield it from Colasurdo with my body. Overtime is four minutes, and I want to use a lot of that clock.

I dribble outside the arc, then bounce the ball to Robin on my left. I yell for the ball right back and Robin cuts inside. Alan gives me a screen and I penetrate, but their center rushes over to me and I have to adjust my shot. It bangs off the rim and they get possession.

Colasurdo has a jump on me, and they get him the ball. He takes it to the hoop and lays it over Peter for two.

I bring it up slowly and they don't press. We work it around outside for about forty-five seconds, until Alan gets around his man inside. Peter gets it to him and Alan hits a fallaway jumper to tie it up again.

There's a lot of passing, a lot of patient offense. We exchange baskets, with them getting a backdoor layup and me getting a put-back on Alan's miss. They call time-out with about forty seconds left.

"One rebound," Alan says. "One defensive stop and then we hold for the last shot. Let's go."

They bring it in. Colasurdo is definitely their best ball-handler, but they don't have any really shaky players like we do. He dribbles outside, watching the movement in the key, and I know he's going to take it in himself.

Suddenly he drives to my left. Alan yells, "Screen," but it's too late. I collide with the guy setting the pick and Colasurdo gets past me. He goes up for the shot and Alan is on him, knocking the ball away.

There's a whistle. The ref points at Alan.

"That's five," Colasurdo says, clapping his hands.

Alan's fouled out. He clasps his hands behind his head and looks at the ceiling. Then he looks at the bench.

Randy and Josh are sitting there, with a combined scoring average of 0.0. Alan waves Randy in, maybe because he has new sneakers. That's the biggest difference between them.

Score's tied. I grab Peter's arm. "Cover their center," I say. "Box out."

Colasurdo goes to the line. Peter and I take the inside spots on the key.

He makes the first one to put them up by a point. The second one bounces high off the back of the rim. I get a hand on it, but can't bring it down. Their big guy taps it back. Colasurdo is standing by the free-throw line. He comes down with the ball and drives the lane. I'm screened and can't get to him.

There's a collision, but the ball is floating toward the hoop. Beth is on her butt, sliding backwards off the court. The shot goes in, but the referee is waving it off, signaling a charging foul on Colasurdo. Beth raises her fists over her head and shouts, "Yeah!"

I walk over and pull her up and we bump shoulders. "You are tough!" I say.

So we're down by a point with nine seconds left, but that's plenty of time, and we *are* going to win. Robin inbounds the ball to me and I dribble up fast. They try to trap me at midcourt but I get through it, take two more dribbles, and shoot.

It hits. Nothing but net, as they say. I put up my fist and holler, and the whole team comes racing over and mobs me. Alan smacks my arm really hard and Beth climbs onto my back. Incredible.

The other team is stone-faced and quiet. The difference between a win and loss in a game like this is immeasurable.

We're back in first place, and we control

our own destiny. We've gotta beat these guys again, and we've gotta beat Kaipo. And we're gonna do it. It's gonna mean something.

FOUR

"Days Later"

"Days Later"

When you said you'd vomited
all day on Saturday
I wished I could have been there
waiting in another room
till you returned
weak and spent
but freshly rinsed
teeth brushed
in need of rest
and sips of water.
I would have fetched it from the kitchen
with an ice cube.

by Jay McLeod

I have this dilemma. There's Spit, who I've
been sleeping with, both literally and figuratively, for about two weeks now. Then
there's Julie, who I haven't seen for that
same two-week span and may never see
again, but who I very much desire to see.

And there's Beth, who has maybe thrown a few signals toward me and would not make a bad girlfriend at all. She's certainly the most stable one of the bunch. I wonder sometimes if I've really made a dent in her consciousness, if she ever thinks about me when I'm not in her presence. I'm thinking I might try to find out.

It's Monday and I'm watching Spit's band practice. They'll be here again all weekend. She catches my eye after a couple of songs and points to the spot next to her on the stage, but I just grin and shake my head. Soon I'll get up there again.

Late at night sometimes I have this fantasy that I'm up there singing for real, belting out some great rock and roll songs before a packed house. And then I go into a lounge singer mode, but classy, and sing some desperate love song directly at Julie to win her over. I figure the odds of that actually happening are about one in fifteen million.

When Spit finishes, she comes over and sits down. "Long time no see," she says. It's been since Thursday.

"It's been brutal without you," I say.

"I bet." She smiles. "You must have been counting the seconds."

I fold my arms. She's in a good mood. This seems like the right time to break this off. It already feels like it never happened.

"So, Spit," I say.

"Yeah?"

"Can we . . . talk about this?"

"This?"

"What we're doing."

"What are we doing?" She gives me a kind of amused look, like she knows what I'm trying to do and knows that it's torture. Then she makes it easy for me. "It's not like I think we're in love," she says.

"No. But . . . it feels kind of destructive. Like we're losing sight of what brought us together in the first place. . . . And it wasn't sex and drugs."

She puts two fingers up to my mouth and pinches my lips. "You're getting smarter, aren't you?"

"Yeah. I guess."

"Okay," she says. "You're off the hook. No more sex buddies. I'll go back to hugging my pillow."

"Hey, the human body can go a good long time, remember?"

She laughs and shakes her head. "Who ever told you *that?*"

I wake up early Tuesday and go play

some ball. It's a slow game — bankers and lawyers, mostly — but Dana and I play our one-on-one game-within-a-game like before. I can see that my play has improved, because she's less effective against me and I'm more so against her. Plus the dynamics have changed a little. I can cover her and bump her without a constant sexual reference point. I can take her on as a basketball player. She's too far over my head to even think about any other relationship.

She says she's jumping well again, having ironed out the kinks. "Five-ten at East Stroudsburg last weekend," she says. "I'm jumping up at Dartmouth on Sunday. Great surface. I may get six feet finally."

She says only five high school girls in the country went six feet or better last year, none of them indoors. "That's my entire focus for the rest of this year," she says. "I'm living like a monk until June."

We don't have a game Thursday night, but I've got nothing to do, so I walk over to the Y anyway. The Presbyterians are warming up on this end. I look around the gym.

"Hey, you," says a very sweet voice, and I see Beth walking toward me. And it isn't so much what she says, but the way she says it: two very distinct words, sort of teasing, but also affectionate and melodic. *Hey, you.*

"Hi," I say. I feel so unencumbered.

"We're up there," she says, pointing to the bleachers. I see Alan, Robin, and Anthony. "We wanted to call you, but nobody knew your number."

"I don't have one."

"Really?"

"Yeah. I live by myself."

"Oh. Somebody told me that. I guess I didn't believe them." She pulls my arm gently. "Come on," she says, and we go up to the bleachers.

Alan and I shake hands by punching each other's fist. He's trying to grow a goatee, but it's pretty sparse. It's as long as the hair on his head, though, which is about a quarter of an inch. I notice that he and Robin are sitting leg to leg, even though there's a lot of room up here.

There are no black girls in our grade, and I think only four in the school. But I've never heard any negative comments about black guys going out with white girls, at least not significant ones. Maybe the parents feel otherwise.

Beth is on my left, and I catch her eye and just tilt my head toward Alan and Robin a little and give a questioning look.

She raises her eyebrows and gives a tiny nod, just a slight bobbing of her head.

Somehow that puts me more at ease, like if two people from the team can pair up, then it's not so unlikely that two more would. I check her out as subtly as I can: lean, strong legs under tight denim, a small pair of old running shoes, nicely rounded —

Bam, the ball rattles off the fourth row of the bleachers because of an errant pass. I jump a little, then laugh. Beth just gives me a look.

After the second game, we head for the door, and Alan says, "Where are we going?"

"The church is open," Robin says. "We could play pool or something."

So we head in that direction. Beth and I lag behind, and the others are soon about a block ahead of us.

"Do you feel like playing pool?" she asks.

"If you want to," I say. "Actually I'm kind of hungry. I was thinking of going to the diner."

"Yeah," she says. "I'm kind of hungry, too."

"You don't mind if we don't catch up to them?"

"No. I'd rather hang with somebody else for a change."

"Yeah?"

"My parents give me a hard time about anybody who isn't into church," she says. "And I don't have the balls to rebel."

She walks real close to me, not with her arm around me or anything, but kind of shoulder to shoulder. When we reach the diner, I ask, "Are you hungry, or did you just say that?"

"I could eat something. I'm not starving."

"Me either."

"Wanna do something else?" she asks.

"Sure."

We walk past the diner and she says we could go to her house. So we walk to the end of Main and turn up Monroe about half a block.

She calls hello to her mom as we enter through the back door. Her mom comes right into the kitchen and says hello.

"This is Jay," Beth says. "From the youth group."

"Hi, Jay," she says. She smiles, but she looks me over good. "Are you new?"

"Yeah. New to the youth group anyway. I been in town awhile."

"Oh. And where do you live?"

"On Main Street."

"North Main?"

"No. By Ninth Street." In other words, in a crummy apartment. There are no houses on the downtown part of Main, just apartments over stores and offices.

We go to the basement and put on the TV, but we don't watch it. She sits about four inches away from me on a couch.

"What's the deal with you living alone?" she asks.

I look up at the ceiling and let out my breath. "They both left," I say. "My mother is . . . not real mature, I guess. She took off when I was little, and she never tried to get me back. My father raised me. He'd been talking about quitting his job and bolting to California for years, but he didn't want to jerk me around any more than I've already been. Last year I told him I was ready to let him go. He thinks I'll be out there with him this summer, but I'm not so sure. He figures eight years as a single parent was more than enough."

"So you really live by yourself?" she asks.

"Yeah. And I work in a bar." I lean in and whisper, "Don't let your mom know."

She giggles. "I'd get grounded just for talking to you."

"I'm bad, huh?"

"You bad." She gives me a punch in the knee.

"So," I say.

"So."

I put my right elbow — the one next to her — up on the back of the couch. It's not exactly a move, but it puts me in position to make one.

"Can you do me a favor?" she asks.

"Sure," I say softly. "Anything."

She blushes a little, looks down. "Well . . . ," she says, "how well do you know Brian Kaipo?"

A Common Thread

Julie shows up around 10 on Friday night as I'm setting a plate of french fries on the bar. We're not real crowded, but I don't think she sees me. I've been finding reasons to be out of the kitchen, watching the door every time it opens.

I see Nancy first, and my chest tightens just a little, my breath halts. Julie's behind her, glancing around. Then her eyes rest on me; there's some acknowledgment. I lean forward and bring a bottle of ketchup up to the bar. "You need anything else?" I say to the guy, who's maybe twenty-five, already losing his hair.

"No thanks," he says.

I tap the bar with my fist and head for the back, not turning to Julie. The band is on a break, sitting at a table near the kitchen. I put a hand on Spit's shoulder. "Can I talk to you a second?" I say.

She follows me into the back.

"Julie's here," I say.

"Oh."

"You think that means anything?"

She laughs. "Of course it does. You think this is the only bar around?"

"It's one of the few she can get into."

"Don't you believe it. She's here 'cause you're here."

I squint a little, put my fingers to my chin. "Yeah, but why? As if I'm the only guy who would be interested in somebody who looks like that? I don't think so."

She shakes her head, gives me that look that says God, you're dense. "You really think that's all there is to it?"

"What?"

"Looks? Maybe she values sincerity or something, or a sense of humor?"

"You mean mine?"

"Yeah, *maybe*."

"She hardly knows me."

"She's not stupid."

"No. She's not."

Spit leans into me, then gently breaks away. "You ever think about why you want *her*? . . . Besides her ass, I mean."

I shrug. "I don't know. Is that the sort of thing I have to answer? I mean, even to myself?"

"No. Not if you're not ready to. But I have a pretty good idea."

"What?"

"She seems like someone you could meet on equal ground. Find some balance; support each other."

We look at each other for a few seconds, one of those understanding looks that secure the bond between us despite everything.

"Listen," she says, "I gotta go back on. Here's the plan." She starts grinning so stupidly that I know she's going to bust my chops, but I'll take it. "You come up onstage with me and I'll go, 'Julie, this young man can't live without you. Do you have it in your heart to forgive him?' Then we'll go into a long medley of Barry Manilow songs until she melts into tears."

"You got it," I say. I must be turning red from blushing, but I love it when she yanks my chain. "Spit?" I say, and she turns from the doorway.

"Yeah?"

"You suck, but thanks."

"You suck, too. You're welcome."

I stay in the kitchen, but Julie doesn't visit this time. I think about things. I will talk to Kaipo, because I like the guy and I think Beth is great. She's made me feel welcome. Maybe I can help her out.

I keep busy. I straighten up the stuff on

the shelves of the walk-in refrigerator, then I sweep the floor and wipe the counters with a rag.

See, I am kind of, I don't know, confused or something. Like right now Julie is the only woman I want, and it feels like I've wanted her forever. But last night I was starting to feel that way about Beth, and I don't have to count backwards very far to find a couple of others. Dana. Maybe that's not so foolish, though. Maybe there's a thread running through this besides my desperation. Maybe they all have something in common. Something like a sense of who they are.

Spit takes another break after 11 and I poke my head out. Julie's over by the jukebox with Nancy, talking to a couple of guys, but her eyes are on the kitchen when I look out. She looks away.

I can't just walk over there and talk to her, because I have to be discreet in here. Deliver food or stay in the kitchen is supposed to be the rule, although I've gotten away with lots more than I ever thought I would. Tonight I think I'll behave.

I go out in the alley for some air. I lean against the brick wall with my arms folded, not really thinking much, just in a state of inertia. It's cold out.

I go in and Julie's standing there, looking at the menu that's taped to the door of the walk-in.

"Hi," I say, sort of tentatively.

"Hi."

She turns to me. And the way I read her face it's softer, but with a line of defense I still need to get through.

"Your friend apologized to me," she says.

"Oh. . . . Can I?"

She tilts her head quickly to the side, then back up. "You can."

"Then I will. I'm sorry."

"It's okay," she says flatly.

"Why'd you come back?"

"I don't know," she says. "Got kicked out of Dinger's."

"Too bad."

"Tell me about it."

There's an edge in her voice that doesn't make this easy, but I figure she's testing me. Maybe I can be funny. "So this was your only option, huh?"

She raises her eyebrows, shakes her head slightly. "No. That's not what I meant at all."

"Oh."

"It was *an* option," she says. "I don't know if it's the right one."

Nancy appears in the doorway, probably according to plan. She gives me a kind of disapproving look, somewhere between amusement and disgust. "You ready?" she says to Julie.

Julie's got her mouth half open, with her tongue peeking out between her teeth. "I guess," she says to Nancy, though she's looking right at me. "We can't stay," she says, this time to me. "I guess I'll see you around."

"You be back tomorrow?"

She shakes her head. "Maybe next week," she says. "We'll see." She starts to go, then gives me a long look. "I'll keep my options open," she says. She finally shows a hint of a smile. "Be good."

Buying Pretzels

The week drags to the point of excruciation, speeding up only during my moments on the basketball court. We beat New Covenant on Sunday, and I go to the church afterward just to avoid being alone in my room. It's okay; I'm not hooked into this church thing, but I'm not repulsed by it either. I'm neutral about it, but it gives me a chance to be around people who actually care about things like school and faith and what their parents think. I stay an hour, talking to Beth mostly, who's fascinated by the fact that I live alone.

Monday I work. Spit comes in all excited.

"Guess where we're playing?" she says.

"Carnegie Hall?"

"Prufrock's."

"What's that?"

She looks surprised that I don't know. "It's a big club. In Scranton. Two weeks from Thursday."

"Great."

"It *is* great. Thursday is big. It's *the* party night in any college town."

Thursdays are big for me, too. This week we play the Cardinals. Next week it's Kaipo. We win them both and we're champions.

"Guess what else?" she says.

"What?"

"They asked me to be an assistant gymnastics coach at the Y. Isn't that cool?"

"Yeah. You going to do it?"

"Definitely, man. Definitely. I love those little kids. I can't wait to get started."

Tuesday morning I wake up abruptly, dreaming about Julie. It's 5:15. I take a quick shower and jog over to the Y, since I'm up anyway.

I go into the gym, but there are only three guys in there. I go down to the weight room and see Dana on the leg-press machine.

"No hoops today?" I ask her.

She looks up and smiles. "No. I think that's it for me," she says. "I can't risk an injury. Things are going too good."

"You clear six?"

"Not quite, but I had three good jumps at it," she says. "I won the meet at five-ten, then had them raise it for me. It's there. It'll happen."

"I'll miss playing against you."

"Yeah. Maybe in the summer." She looks me over for a second, but she's all business. I do a set of pull-ups and some dips. I look over at Dana, eyes shut, benching about 120 pounds. On her way out of this town in a hurry.

The only way to get my mind off Julie is to play basketball. Tuesday night I go back to the Y and get in a pickup game with some old guys in their thirties. They play every week and there's supposedly an age restriction, but they usually need a couple of younger guys to fill out the teams. I stay on the perimeter because there's a lot of beef under the boards and I don't feel like blowing out a knee. It's a slower game than I'm used to, but some of these guys can play. It's fun.

They all head out right at 9, going home to their wives and children. I'm energized from playing, but there's nowhere to go. I walk up to Turkey Hill, get some Gatorade and Yodels, and wonder where everybody is.

Alan and Robin would be together at one of their houses. Beth is probably home doing homework, with Brian on the edge of her consciousness all the time the way Julie is on mine. Spit could be anywhere doing anything, but I think the band is practicing in somebody's basement, getting ready for their breakthrough in Scranton.

Wednesday at lunch, I talk to Kaipo about Beth. He seems interested. Why wouldn't he be?

Thursday takes forever to get here, but it's a definite marker in the week. First, it's game night — a big game, too. Plus it's the night before the weekend, and I'm praying that Julie will be back. If she isn't, then next week will be more unbearable than this one was.

We've got the first game, so I can put in a good warm-up in a near-empty gym. I show up an hour early and get moving slowly, shooting chippies and free throws before working up to more intense stuff. The path is clear: we win our next three (tonight, Sunday against the Baptists, and next Thursday against Kaipo) and we clinch the league. We lose tonight or next week — or worse, lose both — and we're in trouble.

Players from both teams start trickling in, and my energy level starts to build. I can block out everything for this hour on the court, exhaust myself, drain my emotions, cleanse my psyche.

And I play my best game of the season. I own the lane, driving in and either beating my man for layups or nailing short fallaway jumpers. We build a double-digit lead in the first half and never let them in it.

They put two players on me in the second half, but I keep finding the open man, which is usually Beth or Robin. They both get a couple of layups and the game turns into a blowout.

I can rest easy tonight, for once.

Friday night arrives and I'm pumped. I keep the kitchen clean, wiping down the stove after every hamburger, planning for an early escape if something happens. She's never shown up before 9, and usually not until 10, but tonight could be different. She could be as distracted as I am.

Spit comes on about 9:30. She's sounding good. There's a big loud crowd. People start dancing right away and I've got lots of energy flowing again, like right before last night's game.

I make myself stay in the back because I want her to come to me. This is my territory. But by 10 I figure she ought to be here, so I look out and around. She isn't.

I go out in the alley, talking to myself. It's about twenty degrees tonight, but I'm pumping out a lot of heat. I walk back and forth a few times, jump straight up in the air, and go back inside.

I try to keep busy, but there isn't much to do. I keep checking out the bar room, but Julie never shows. By midnight I'm depleted. I don't know where all the energy went, because I haven't done anything but cook, wash dishes, and wait for her.

I shut down the kitchen, watch the band for a few minutes, then go upstairs to bed.

I don't want to go through this again tomorrow.

Saturday afternoon I walk over to the Y. There's little-kid soccer going on in the gym, so I go down to the weight room, which is basically alien ground to me. I do some pull-ups, a couple of sets of bench presses, and about fifty crunches, then spend twenty minutes on an exercise bike.

Soccer's over by the time I head upstairs, and there's already a three-on-three half-court basketball game under way. There's a couple of guys from the Cardinals waiting in the bleachers, so I team with them to play against the winners.

I play about an hour, then quit because I have to go to work. I'm psyched up from playing hoops, feeling good. But as I head down the steps, it hits me like an orange: if Julie doesn't show up tonight, she won't ever.

I remain stoic throughout the early evening, doing my job, thinking ahead to tomorrow night's game, cooking wings, listening to the jukebox. There is a chance, however slight, that I will join Spit onstage toward the end of the night. If Julie doesn't show, I'll say screw this and leave the old me behind, getting up there and singing, maybe more than even the choruses. I don't tell Spit that I'm thinking this, but I feel like I've got an open invitation.

My voice sucks? So what, it's the only one I've got.

Shorty comes limping into the back about ten to 9.

"I need you to run to the store," he says.

"Which one?"

"The supermarket." He's handing me a twenty. "We got no pretzels," he says. "I don't know how the hell I let that happen, but I did. Take my truck. It's out back."

I won't make it to the market in town in time, so I head out to the twenty-four-hour place on Route 6. I hardly ever drive, but

Shorty's truck is a piece of shit so I'm not too worried. He's got a Lynyrd Skynyrd tape in, so I listen to "Free Bird" live on the way out.

I figure I should spend the whole twenty, which yields ten assorted bags of Sturgis, Rold Gold, and Snyder's.

The band is on by the time I get back. I make two trips to the bar with the pretzels. I'm walking back to the kitchen after the second trip, when Julie steps out of the bathroom.

Ironically, the pretzel trip had put her out of my head for the first time all week. We lock eyes and my face gets warm because I sense that hers does. Her look says that she's happy to see me and that she doesn't want to let on that she is.

"Hey, stupid," she says.

"Hey . . . you."

"How's the hamburger business?"

"Great. How's waitressing?"

"It's a living."

She's friendly again, sort of like before. But I'm no better at reading her than I ever was. Either way, I don't want this to be the last time I see her, and I don't want another uncertain week like this last one. So I muster up all the courage I have, which is just barely enough to nod my head toward the kitchen. "Come on," I say. "I wanna talk to you."

"Okay," she says. "I can listen."

I'm struck again by how cute she is — the tight, athletic body; the eyes that hold me when we speak — but that also makes me think about what Spit said, why I want her besides what she looks like. And I think in part it's the mystery, the fact that I really don't know much about her, even though I like what I see. But there's a lot more to it than that. Like Spit said: I think we're in a similar place, or maybe just emerging from one.

"I like you," I say.

She nods slowly, a firm little smile on her lips. "That's good."

No breakthrough yet.

"I *really* like you," I say. "I was scared to death I'd never see you again."

She shrugs. "Well, here I am."

I let out my breath. "I know. But what I don't know is why."

"Why not?"

"I mean, are you here because of me, or do I just happen to be here?"

She tilts her head slightly. Her mouth softens. "You."

The word comes out rounded; it hits me

like a bullet and spreads through my chest. This is a first — a bigger first than what happened with Brenda or Spit, or what might have happened with Julie the first time around.

I sense a wall coming down. She's leaning against the sink, and her smile no longer has that glint of ice in it. And suddenly I don't really want her here, because I don't want her to be some chick who has to chase after some guy in a bar.

So I do a manly thing and set up a barrier for myself, another stick for me to jump over. "Would you want to go out sometime?" I ask. "Like for real?"

She looks me up and down. "I might," she says. "We were headed in that direction once."

"I know. I didn't intend to get sidetracked."

"I didn't either."

We stare at each other for a few long seconds. I'm thinking Shorty would let me borrow his truck some weeknight. "So?" I ask.

"That would be nice," she says. "I'll give you my number."

She leaves soon after, and I don't make any attempt to touch her. I think she got what she came for, and I know I did, too.

255

I'm still confused as shit, but I'm happy as hell. I wouldn't trade that combination for anything.

LEFTOVER RICE

Sunday whips by because all the pressure is off me. I'm absolutely flying all morning, like I could probably get my hand above the rim, and I can't wait to get on the basketball court.

I stayed up late last night, staring at the phone number written by Julie's own hand, dancing by myself to a Steve Earle tape, and breathing in the sweet, cold air coming through my wide-open window. I finally crashed at 4 and woke up this morning around 9.

The Y opens at 10 on Sunday, and there are half-court games going on all day. I get a late breakfast at the diner and walk over there, ready to play for two or three hours, even though we've got a game tonight. I can run all day, so I've got no concern about tiring myself out. Plus a half-court game is more about passing and cutting. All it'll do is help me settle down, get into a groove that should carry over to tonight.

The phone call will happen tomorrow

evening. Shorty's already agreed to the use of his truck, so I'm figuring a movie the following Monday, since I'll be working and playing hoops most of the week. I'd ask her to one of my games, but she'd be too much of a distraction.

Playing this afternoon is the right thing to do, because I'm overpumped and my first couple of games suck as a result. But I do get settled after a while and start playing well. The mix of players ranges from freshmen up to about age forty, and the skill range is at least that wide. I don't do anything stupid like challenge the big guys underneath. I'm more concerned about an injury than getting tired, so I play a true point guard position, controlling the offense, but mostly looking for assists.

Life goes in cycles; I know that. I'm starting an up cycle now, and I've earned it. And I know the things that are happening now will help me through the next downturn, which will be unavoidable and strengthening.

I see in the paper that the Weston CC team is 2–17, so there might be room for me next year. Kaipo is definitely going, so I figure I'll apply. I'm sure not going anywhere else.

I eat my second meal of the day about 4,

just a couple of cans of tuna fish in my room, an orange, a cucumber, some left-over rice from the Chinese take-out place, and half a box of cookies. We don't play until 7, the third game, so I set my alarm for 6 and lie down for a nap.

We don't say much, warming up. Everybody knows what's at stake, everybody knows these guys embarrassed us last time.

Alan points to the Baptists as we huddle up before the game. "That is the most patient, team-oriented team in the league," he says, "and if we let down tonight, they'll send us packing again. We're at least thirty points better than they are. Let's show it."

"You guys starting?" Beth asks.

"Yeah," Alan says. "We're starting."

I don't shoot at all the first few times we have possession, working it around, finding Alan and Robin inside for a pair of layups apiece. Next time up, I fake a pass to the corner and drive, hitting a soft jumper in the lane to make it 10–4. They call time-out.

"Let's press," I say in the huddle. "Just a couple of times, just me and Peter. Let's put them away early."

Alan nods. "Okay," he says. "Next basket. Press, but don't foul."

They don't expect it. Peter tips the inbounds pass and I grab it, laying it up off the backboard. We go right back into the press, and they try a pass to midcourt to break it. Beth steps in and intercepts it. We pull it back out, work it around, and Robin hits Alan inside for an easy layup. We're up by twelve and everything's clicking. By halftime, we've built it to twenty.

"Now we'll sit," Alan says. "Peter play the pivot, Beth bring up the ball. Play tough, deliberate defense and work for good shots on offense. Jay and I will give you some rests, but I want you guys to do the work. Let's go."

It's not the prettiest half of basketball, but we maintain the lead and you can see some confidence developing. I go in and play center for about three minutes, which is fun. I can get up higher than any of their players, so I snag a bunch of rebounds.

We're ready for Thursday. We win and we're in. If Kaipo's team beats us, we'll be tied with one game to play, and it'd almost definitely come down to a play-off. I don't want to let that happen.

The Sound in My Head

I decide not to call Julie from the bar. I want to disassociate this relationship from that place. So I take a break and go over to the diner.

A guy who I assume is her father answers.

"Is, uh, is Julie there?" I say.

"Hold the wire." I hear him set the phone down, then there's silence for about a minute until she picks up.

"It's Jay," I say.

"Hey," she says, and I don't hear any challenge in her voice. She sounds glad to hear from me. "What's going on?"

"Not much," I say. "I wanted to, you know, set something up. You said you'd want to go out sometime."

"Sure. When?"

"Well, because of work and all, I'm pretty busy this week. But maybe a week from tonight. Is that all right?"

"Let me think. Yeah, that's great. I mean, I'll have to have another uncle die or

261

something, but I'll work it out."

"Okay. Would a movie be okay?"

"Sure."

"Okay." I let go of my breath. "Good."

"Great. You want to get together before that?" she asks.

"Yeah. I want to."

"You don't work Saturday afternoon, do you?"

"No. Not until about five."

"I'll come pick you up," she says. "Like at noon. We can hang out. Whatever."

"Great," I say. "That's great."

"Yeah," she says. "I think it will be."

Thursday. Beth arrives at the gym with Kaipo, and she's hanging on his arm. Alan and I go over, and Alan waves her toward him and says, "Later." He shakes hands with Brian, who gives him a playful shove on the shoulder.

Brian and I smack hands. "Good luck," he says.

"You too."

Alan sort of drags Beth down to our end of the gym.

We're quiet while we warm up, but very focused. My energy level is high, and I'm working to control it. I take a lot of jump shots, and follow up the misses with high, leaping put-backs.

Robin and Beth tie their hair back. Alan goes down to the locker room to throw up.

The bleachers are getting full. Somebody brought in a boom box and it's playing some rap shit.

I just want this game to get started.

Alan waves us over to the bench, and we huddle around him as he stares at the floor. "This game means a lot to me," he says. "It means a lot to all of you, and to the guys on the other team. It may mean something to the other players in the league. . . . It means absolutely nothing to anyone else in the world." He looks up, catches my eyes, then Peter's, then Beth's. "Do you give a shit? Do you want this thing as much as I do? . . . Let's kick some ass."

We all put our fists together and shout "Let's go!" louder than we ever have, with an edge.

We're maybe too intense in the opening minutes, too physical, hustling just a little more than we need to. We make a few sloppy plays, but we keep it even. The problem is the fouls. I draw one and Alan gets two before the first quarter is half over.

"You guys," Beth says during a time-out, shaking her head. "We lose one of you and forget it."

"We'll settle down," Alan says.

I wipe my face with the front of my shirt. My legs are tired. I never expected that.

I get in a shooting zone in the second quarter, hitting a couple of short jumpers and a long one. Kaipo's had only one steal from me, and I've kept him from shooting as much as he normally would. But he's getting it inside to Robinson, who's only hit a couple of baskets, but did draw those fouls on Alan.

Kaipo crosses midcourt with the ball and I guard him close. I don't go for the steal because he almost always drives past me when I do. But I have to keep the pressure on, keep him from getting an open shot, even from twenty feet out.

He gets it in to Robinson, but Alan's got him covered good and Peter slides over to help. Kaipo drifts toward the baseline and I race to stay with him. Robinson gets him the ball and he goes up with it, shooting it over my outstretched hand and sinking it cleanly. They're up by two.

Alan inbounds the ball to me, and I take a quick breath as I start to dribble. "Watch it," Alan yells, but it's too late. Kaipo flicks it out of my hands and drives to the hoop. Alan darts over and tries to draw a charge, but Kaipo slips cleanly past him and banks it in for two more.

They hadn't been pressing, but I should have been ready. Alan slaps the ball between his hands and passes in to me, and I shield it with my body this time. When I turn, I see Kaipo at midcourt, with a hint of a smile on his face.

"How much time?" I yell, as I dribble past the scorer's table.

"Less than a minute."

I decide that we should hold it for the last shot of the half. We can't see the clock, but the scorer gives you a "Twenty . . . fifteen . . . ten" warning at the end of every quarter.

I wave Alan out from underneath and pass him the ball. We work it around the perimeter, killing time, but everybody knows I need to end up with it. Alan has the ball at "Fifteen," and I run over and get it. I dribble to the top of the key with Kaipo on me tight, keeping my shoulder in his face, protecting the ball.

I feint right, then drive into the lane with Kaipo all over me. I pop up, drifting away. All I see is blue shirt, but I get the shot off as he makes contact with my arm.

The shot goes in. The foul's called, too, and I make the free throw to cut the lead to a point at halftime.

We head for the bench, but Alan says, "Downstairs," so we follow him down the narrow back stairway. He pokes his head in the men's locker room, but then comes out. He looks at Robin. "Check the women's room," he says.

She does. "It's empty," she says, so we go in there and sit down. I get a quick look at Spit's mural, which is vivid and impressive.

"Great half," Alan says. "We're going to a modified zone on defense. Jay, you stay on Kaipo. Peter, you take Robinson. Stay in his face. If he gets past you, I'm there, but don't give him an open jumper. I'll kill them off the boards if you can keep him away from the basket. Robin and Beth, you play the wings. Don't get caught in a screen."

"Don't worry if they get a guy loose in the corner," I say. "They've only got two guys who can hit that consistently — Brian and Robinson. And if Robinson plays outside, they've got nothing underneath."

Alan sticks his fist out and we all put ours out, too. "All right," he says, "let's go. We own this league. Let's do it."

★ ★ ★

The strategy works. Robinson tries to take advantage of the mismatch with Peter, but his shooting is off and Alan keeps getting rebounds. You can see Robinson's anger growing; he's throwing lots of elbows. We build the lead to four, then seven. Alan and I are doing all of the scoring, but the other three know their roles, when to come to the ball, just how to feed it to Alan.

Late in the quarter, I nail a jumper from deep in the corner to extend the lead to eight. I pump my fist as we run downcourt. Kaipo takes the ball and dribbles up slowly. The relaxed, sort of amused look he usually has on his face in these games is gone, replaced with a hardened intensity. He crosses midcourt, takes two quick dribbles, and unleashes a twenty-five footer that swishes cleanly.

I bring it up, work it inside to Alan again, and he pivots and scores. The lead is seven.

Kaipo dribbles up, reaches the same spot as before, and promptly hits another one, never even bothering to look inside. The lead is four. We get another layup. He hits another bomb. The lead is three.

I make a bad pass, and one of their guys

knocks it clear. Brian gets control and I pick him up in the backcourt. No more open shots.

Ten seconds left in the quarter. I guard him tight. He starts to drive and I back-pedal and stumble. He sets up and shoots.

The lead is gone.

"Damn," Alan says as we get to the bench. "You want to switch?" he asks me, meaning should he guard Kaipo instead?

I shake my head. "No. We're still out-playing them. The offense is working. I'll shut him down."

Alan looks at Josh and Randy, who haven't played a second. He takes a deep breath. "Beth. Take a short rest. Randy, you come in. You've got one assignment, and one assignment only. Harass the shit out of Brian in the backcourt. You won't get a steal, but you might get on his nerves a little.

"Beth, you and Josh report in after two minutes for Robin and Randy. Josh, you do exactly what I told Randy to do. You guys don't have to foul him, just slow him down a little. Jay, you pick up at half-court."

The Randy Press is about equivalent to having a mosquito harass an elephant, but it does get Kaipo out of his rhythm, if only slightly. He scores the first basket of the quarter, but this time it's only worth two points and we make him work a little harder to get it.

I dribble up very deliberately. I've had some good stretches of basketball this season, some good ones tonight. But these final eight minutes better be like nothing I've ever done before.

Kaipo picks me up at midcourt. I watch the movement inside, with Peter and Alan struggling to get free. Kaipo's all over me, and I do a dumb thing and stop my dribble. They immediately double-team me, but I hear Robin yelling and somehow bounce the ball to her. She's got an open lane and she drives, but Robinson comes out and cuts her off. She makes a nice pass to Alan, who's open underneath, and he banks it home to tie the game at 47.

Kaipo hits his sixth straight bucket, I make a driving layup, and he comes back and hits another. Alan calls time-out. Josh and Beth report in.

"Two minutes' rest, Robin," Alan says. "Jay, keep chasing that man."

"I'm playing him full-court the rest of the way," I say.

"How much time is left?" Peter asks.

"Lots," Alan says. "Suck it up."

I slow it down a little. Kaipo's too hot; I've got to break his momentum. I get it in to Alan, and he goes up and pounds it in over Robinson, getting fouled in the process. The free throw gives us back the lead, 52–51.

I press, not going for the steal, but wanting to make Kaipo work for every inch. Then it happens, that rare mistake. He switches hands and slightly loses control, just enough for me to poke a hand in there and knock the ball away. It bounces toward our basket and we scramble toward it. I get a hand on it first, slide onto a knee, and come up with it, maintaining a dribble and stepping toward the hoop. Kaipo's off balance and can't help fouling me as I shoot. The ball goes in anyway.

Alan and I slap hands hard as I walk to the foul line. "You make this sucker," he says.

And I do. A four-point lead is big. We can win this.

I stay in Brian's face. I've got this man now, I know every move. He makes a pass inside, cuts on the give-and-go, takes it back, and goes up for a jumper. And I know it's coming, I know where it's going.

I time my jump right, get my hand up, and deflect the ball out of bounds.

Alan comes over. We bump chests. He's steaming.

I stay glued to Kaipo. Robinson inbounds the ball to their other guard, who hasn't touched it in I don't know how long. He loses control and Alan grabs it. He cradles it in his arms. I can hear his fierce breathing as I take it from him and dribble.

The thing you've gotta know about basketball is that you can play as hard as you want, fight for every rebound, dive for every loose ball, run your ass off up and down the court, but you still have to put the ball in the basket. Shooting the ball through a hoop from eighteen feet away with a man in your face and the pressure on your shoulders is not an easy task in any situation. But somehow you do it, somehow you really can will it to happen. Somehow you don't allow it *not* to.

Alan scores again. Robinson takes a time-out with us up by six. Alan tells Robin to get back in there. Four more minutes and we're champions.

We don't say much. I'm breathing heavy, my shirt is soaked, but I'm not tired, not at all. In fact, I have to tell myself to stay in control, to not overplay these last few minutes, to not let myself get burned.

We exchange baskets, with Alan getting a pair of layups and Robinson and Kaipo hitting one apiece. Next time up, Brian plays off me a bit, ready to get inside and help out on Alan, who's been unstoppable this half. I get greedy, I shoot the three. It bangs off the rim, and Kaipo soars for the rebound. He comes down on the run, and I'm caught flat-footed. He goes the length of the court and lays it in. It's 61–57.

Kill some time, I tell myself. Be patient. I make safe passes, first to Peter, then Robin, coming right back to them and retaking the ball. When Alan gets open, he's getting the ball. If he doesn't get open I'm keeping it.

Kaipo finally fouls me. I turn and yell, "Time?"

"One-twenty," comes the reply.

I sink the first one, miss the second. Robinson comes down with the rebound. Alan stays in his face.

Kaipo hits a three. I dribble up and look inside for Alan, then drive to the hoop, drawing Kaipo and Robinson to me. I spot Peter wide open underneath and send him a soft bounce pass. He fields it and makes the easy layup, the only player other than me or Alan to score for us this half.

It's 64–60 and there's about half a minute to play. Kaipo knows they need two scores. He won't force a three-pointer, but he'll take it if it's there. Most important is to make him eat some time.

I hound him good, not giving him a path to the basket. He's looking patient, but I know he's aware of the clock. When he starts his drive, I stay with him. I hear Alan yell, "Screen," and I collide with Robinson near the free-throw line. He shoves me off, the ref blows his whistle, and I figure that has to be an offensive foul. But the call is on Alan instead, who fouled Kaipo as he went up for a shot.

That's four on Alan, but that won't be a factor unless we go to overtime.

Kaipo hits both free throws, and they go into a furious full-court press, desperate to get the ball back. Nine seconds left and we're up by two. They either have to steal it or foul somebody. Alan takes the ball out-of-bounds under their basket and looks at Peter. I yell "No!" and Alan turns toward me. Kaipo's all over me, but Alan manages to get me the ball and I'm immediately fouled.

I take a deep breath and walk the length of the court to the free-throw line. Seven seconds left. No matter what I do, Kaipo is going to go down and hit a three-pointer. If I miss this shot, they'll win the game. If I make the first I'll get a second one, and the best they could do is send it to overtime. If I make them both, it's over.

I bounce the ball three times slowly, concentrating on the rim. The sound of the spectators, the breathing of the guys waiting for the rebound, the rubbing of my fingers on the ball as I shut my eyes and inhale, it all finally matches the sound in my head, it all fits together.

Kaipo's to my right, coiled and intense. I let it fly, softly over the rim, and it swishes cleanly through the net.

The referee slaps the ball back to me and I take another breath and three more dribbles. I squeeze the ball into a universe and send it toward the basket, and I know from the moment of release that it will make it.

I put up my fist as the ball ripples the net and holler, "Don't foul!"

We're up by four. They don't have time to catch us.

Kaipo takes the long inbounds pass, dribbles three times on the run, and cleanly hits a twenty-eight-footer as the final whistle blows. Not enough. We win it.

Alan embraces me. Robin and the others

run toward us, yelling and pumping their fists.

Kaipo smacks my shoulder. "Hell of a game," he says.

"You're the man."

Beth hugs me and kisses my cheek, and Kaipo smacks hands with me again. "Most fun I ever had on a basketball court," he says. "Great job."

Kaipo's played bigger games before, and he'll play plenty of others. This one may be out of his head in an hour, but it sure won't be out of mine.

Alan and I had our highest-scoring games of the season. I scored thirty-one and Alan had twenty-nine. Kaipo finished with forty-two, but we made him work for every point.

Alan and I go downstairs and sit on the bench in the locker room. He keeps shaking his head, going, "Awesome game. Just awesome."

I peel off my T-shirt and shut my eyes, still breathing hard. "Now what?" I say.

"Celebrate, man. They got a party set up at the church."

"Oh." I nod. I guess that'll be okay for an hour. "Hey."

"What?"

"You sure you want to go to Yale?"

He laughs, hesitates a second. "Yeah. Yeah, I do. I can play intramural. And there's a summer league here. I'll get enough basketball."

"There's never enough basketball," I say.

He stands and starts getting undressed. "Let's get out of here," he says. "I'm psyched. That was awesome tonight, man. Just awesome."

Riding Seaward

I hang at the church for a while. They've got soda and cake and stuff. They invited everybody from the league to come by, and most people did.

I'm standing with Alan when Kaipo and Beth come in holding hands. Alan whacks him on the arm. "No Catholics allowed," he says.

"I'm an honorary Methodist now," Brian says, holding up Beth's hand as evidence.

"You wish," Alan says. "This is the church of champions."

Brian laughs. "Yeah. You kicked our butts."

They joke around some more. I mostly listen. I'll never be at home in this place, but I like walking through the light now and then.

When I decide to leave, I shake hands with Alan and some other guys. I want to get out. I hope I can find Spit, because I owe her a lot and I want to be with her.

I walk up to North Main Street into the

wind and turn up a side street toward her house. I fully expect to find her; I don't know why. And as I turn onto her block, I see her approaching from the opposite direction.

"Hey," I say.

"Hey."

"Where you been?"

"Mike's. From the band. Just jamming."

"We won," I tell her.

"Cool. I figured you would."

"How come?" I ask.

" 'Cause you deserved to."

"Yeah? That's not how it usually works."

"Yeah, it does. You get what you earn, one way or another. That time I saw you play I couldn't believe how good you were. It was pure."

I shuffle my feet around, reach up and touch her face during the pause. "You wanna hear something stupidly poetic I've been thinking about?" I ask. "I mean, you might be able to turn it into a song or something."

She sticks her bare hands into her pockets. "Yeah. Shoot."

I blush and laugh. "I feel like I've been circling around this thing, this heat source, getting close to it three or four times and then blasting far away from it, almost out of orbit. But now I'm feeling the heat again. Feeling like I might even touch down."

She just gives me that goofy smile of hers. She gives me a gentle push in the chest.

"Pretty stupid, huh?" I say.

"I don't know," she says. "When you get too close to the heat, you get burned, but I'd rather get toasted than frozen."

"Yeah. How's the sessions going?"

"Good. We'll be ready." The Prufrock's thing is a week away. I know she's been nervous as hell.

We're both kind of glowing. We're back where we were before, before we got our bodies tangled up and were just allowing our minds to engage.

"I still want to get on stage with you," I say. "I wanna get up there and do it."

"Anytime, babe," she says. "Anytime you're ready."

"I'll be ready soon," I say. "I think the time is coming."

"Just say the word," she says. "You don't have to rush it." She brushes my hair from my forehead, then shakes back her own hair and smiles. "You'll come with us to Prufrock's? Help us set up and all? I think I'll be better if you're there."

"Yeah. I'm there. Think we can sneak Julie in, too?"

"I don't see why not. Can she sing some backup?"

"I don't know."

We start walking back down Main Street. I feel like I'm floating, like I've won an Olympic medal or something. I mean, we won the league, I'm in good with Julie, and Spit and I have reached a better level of friendship. We walk past Turkey Hill and the banks, and hang out in front of the pizza place. I see Alan and Robin and Beth and some others in there, but we don't go in. We stay on the sidewalk and listen to the sound of human voices. People laughing.

Spit starts singing. I listen carefully.

I listen so I'll learn all the words.